The Breeze

Also by Eddie L. Barnes:

The Legacy of the Desperado (self-published)
Western Tales and Such (self-published)
The Bar-B-Que Circuit
The Diary of a Gunfighter
The Breeze

The Breeze

—Continued—

Eddie L. Barnes

iUniverse LLC
Bloomington

THE BREEZE
The Bar-B-Que Circuit, Continued

This is a work of fiction. All of the characters, names, incidents, organizations, and dialogue in this novel are either the products of the author's imagination or are used fictitiously.

iUniverse books may be ordered through booksellers or by contacting:

iUniverse LLC
1663 Liberty Drive
Bloomington, IN 47403
www.iuniverse.com
1-800-Authors (1-800-288-4677)

ISBN: 978-1-4917-1389-1 (sc)
ISBN: 978-1-4917-1391-4 (hc)
ISBN: 978-1-4917-1390-7 (e)

Library of Congress Control Number: 2013920808

Printed in the United States of America.

iUniverse rev. date: 12/09/2013

Contents

This book is dedicated to David Bonner (left) of Amarillo, Texas. I think he actually helped invent the Bar-B-Que Circuit, at least the one in the panhandle of Texas. If he didn't invent the circuit, then in my opinion, he certainly was the chairman of the board. He has more snap than any person I have ever known. And another thing . . . I have never in my life heard anyone say anything derogatory about David. That speaks well for any man.

I have always felt he could have qualified for the Senior Professional Golf Association Tour had he not taken ill. The illness certainly came too early in his life. He is a unique, talented person I am proud to call a friend. I am certainly enriched for having him call me a friend.

He was always fast with a quip. We once played a golf tournament on a course in rather poor condition. When David complained to the golf professional, he was told, "It's the same for everyone, so what's the big deal?" David replied, "Well, it's the same for everyone getting one up the old gazoo, but it doesn't make it fun!"

I wish him well for the rest of his life.

Acknowledgments

Thanks to Clyde Foch Posey (what a great teacher he was), Larry Chapman, Stan Bush, Royce Woolard, Harry and John Bettis, Harry Bettis, Mac Woodfin, Roland Adams, David Bailey, Ben Brock, Roy Deaton, Jimmie Wilson, Captain Jay Ellis, Ray Fendley, Robert Cleland, and especially David Bonner.

Thanks to the countless, wonderful crazies who made me laugh so hard my eyes would water.

Introduction

Golf—a gentleman's game. Really!

In my formative years learning the game of golf, I found it anything but.

Genteel? No way! There was always someone wanting to personally challenge me, to relieve me of my hard-earned money, or to simply brag they were better.

Well, who was going to know? The world?

No, just a few other ne'er-do-wells willing to listen for the price of a free cocktail or a cold beer.

"Yeah, man, I kicked his ass!"

Well, not really. You only beat me playing golf.

Some of those ne'er-do-wells would do anything to win, thereby sacrificing all integrity: tee up a ball in the rough, move it from a bad lie in the fairway, mark it closer to the hole on the green . . . You know, anything for an edge. It only revealed their lack of talent.

Can anyone call those actions gentlemanly? The resulting conflicts were certainly not genteel. In past times, conflicts between two parties were sometimes settled by a duel. People say it was the gentlemen's way. How could getting shot be gentlemanly?

These things still happen even today, and at the finest of private clubs.

I had fun learning the game of golf: practicing the art, competing, and sometimes winning in spite of those distractions.

Actually, I never had fun during the actual playing of a golf competition. It was work if I wanted to do my best, filled with stress. I liked it, but it wasn't fun.

The fun came afterward—fun from the satisfaction if you played well. Euphoria if you won. And of course, there were always the camaraderie of friends, the soothing effect of alcohol, and the riotous characters one encountered on the Bar-B-Que Circuit.

Just like the characters in this book.

The little white ball, lying on the ground,
Wonder why till now, it hasn't been found?
Oh so lonely, lying there all alone,
I'll take it with me, give it a new home.
Little white ball, lying on the ground,
It once was lost, but is now found.
Tee it up, and give it a resounding whack,
The distance is good, but direction it lacks!
Out into the weeds, where it had been,
The search is futile, oh my, lost again.
Lying somewhere, lonely, on the ground,
Little ball, waiting, silently, hoping to be found.

CHAPTER 1

Eloy Baines loaded his golf clubs into the two-toned-rust and rose-colored-1979 Cadillac Seville, then got into the driver's seat, lit a cigarette, and put the car in motion.

He had just finished playing in the Gaines County Open in Seminole, Texas, and had played decent, but not good.

He took his usual way home from the Gaines County Country Club to Midland. From the Gaines County Country Club, it was south on Highway 62/385 though the town of Seminole, left on Fairfield, and then a quick right onto Telephone Road. Telephone Road was a two-lane county road that eventually became Highway 1788 leading straight to Midland.

Simple trip, but some didn't like to go this way because part of the road was open range—livestock had the right of way.

The other element of danger was the road was pitch-black this night. It was overcast and cloudy, no light of moon to light the way.

Eloy took a sip from a Styrofoam cup filled with scotch.

He removed a Marlboro from its package, reached over, punched in the cigarette lighter, waited for it to pop out, and then lit the cigarette.

The glare from the red-hot lighter momentarily blinded Eloy, and when he recovered, he thought he saw a man in the middle of the road—waving his arms!

Eloy reacted instinctively to avoid the collision. He swerved to the right, but not in time.

The impact of the collision sent the Cadillac careening into the bar ditch on the right side of the road. The car slammed into the side of the steep ditch and leaned hard left onto the two left-side tires. The car was racing along in the bar ditch and Eloy was fighting for control—fighting to keep the car from rolling over. Finally, the bank on the right side became flatter and the car slammed back to all four tires.

Eloy slammed on the brakes.

He tried to get out of the car, but the driver-side door wouldn't open. He slid across the seat and got out of the passenger side to assess the damage.

The entire left side of the two-toned-rust and rose-colored-1979 Cadillac Seville looked like it had been peeled off with a can opener.

The left side of the hood was crumpled and bent backward, almost to the left wheel.

The left front wheel was crooked and bent.

Eloy went to look for the person he had hit—who he had just possibly killed. He searched and searched but couldn't find anyone. *What the hell just happened?*

He went back to his car, got a flashlight, and gave it a close inspection. He found cowhide hair on what was once the left-side mirror.

He found more cowhide on the rear bumper.

Eloy breathed a heavy sigh of relief.

He had hit a cow, not a person. The arms he thought he saw waving in the air were actually the cow's horns. He wouldn't have to go to jail after all. But he might be in trouble with some rancher since this was open range and all damages to livestock had to be paid.

He got back in the car and slowly drove up and down the road for a couple of miles but couldn't find the cow. *Good for me,* he thought. *I just saved myself a thousand dollars or so.*

He slowly drove the car back to Midland. The bent wheel on the left front prevented any speed more than twenty miles per hour.

He was so scared he forgot to see if he had shit his pants.

Eloy called a wrecker the next morning and had the Cadillac taken from his house to the dealership for an estimate on the repair cost.

He was told the car was totaled. The radiator and air-conditioning units had suffered damage and the cost to repair them was more than the car was worth.

Eloy bade the Cadillac good-bye and then purchased the car he had always wanted—a new 1985 red Mercedes 450SL convertible—red hard top and black soft top.

He thought back on the incident that could have killed him. If he had not been lighting the cigarette, he might have seen the animal sooner and avoided the collision.

He quit smoking, cold turkey, at that moment.

Eloy drove around town while enjoying his new Mercedes and decided to play golf in the Monday game at Hogan Park Municipal Golf Course.

The Monday game at Hogan Park was a big game, sometimes with thirty to forty players. They would stand around the putting green and make up teams. The bets were usually all Nassau's, so they could settle them quicker after the round. Eloy liked the Nassau bets, a bet on the front nine score, a bet on the back nine score, and a bet for the total score.

John Echard was there, so Eloy was hoping it would be a good day. John could play really well at Green Tree Country Club, but take him to any other course, and usually it was *poof!* Complete hacker.

This day, it turned out to be just the opposite of what he had thought. It was a bad day for Eloy and a good day for John. John said he would come by Eloy's house and settle the bets.

When Eloy turned onto his street later that day, he noticed Himey Wilkinson's car parked in front of his house. That wasn't unusual. It was parked there quite often.

Eloy pulled the red Mercedes convertible into his driveway, opened the garage door, and parked on the right side of the two-car garage. He opened the trunk, removed his clubs, and sat them on the floor beside the car. He unzipped the side pocket, removed a bank bag, and removed four twenty-dollar bills.

He had to pay John Echard, of all people, and his mood was sour.

Eloy had not played very good golf since he'd hurt his back twelve months ago while qualifying for the Texas State Amateur Championships. He had been playing his best golf ever and would have qualified, had it not happened.

On the last qualifying hole, he had bent over to tee his ball, and when he had tried to stand, he couldn't.

He walked to a storage cabinet and removed some rope. He tied a hangman's noose with the rope.

He walked back to his golf bag, slipped the noose around the bag, and hung it from the center rafter. "Treasonous bastards," he said aloud.

He then made his way into the house, through the laundry room, and into the kitchen. He poured a few ounces of Macallan over two ice cubes. He knew you weren't supposed to pour Macallan over ice. The Macallan distillers told him the ice changed the scotch's molecular structure. He didn't know what the molecular structure had to do with anything, because when you drank it with ice or without, it still made you drunk.

He walked out of the kitchen, into the great room, and then onto the covered patio, looking for Himey. He heard noises coming from the hot tub area.

Eloy walked to the privacy fence and peered over the edge. He saw Himey Wilkinson and Echard's wife, Megan, both naked, in the hot tub.

When Megan saw Eloy, she stood, bent over, and shook her butt at Eloy.

There it was, plain as day. It looked like a black cat with its tongue hanging out.

Mega looked hot, inviting, and Eloy thought about joining the party, but he resisted.

Himey waved at Eloy with his right hand. His left hand was holding a Miller Lite.

"You'd better figure an exit strategy, son. John is due here in about twenty minutes," said Eloy. Then he grinned.

He turned and left, trying to think of a diversion to keep a murder from happening in his house.

He sat and drank his scotch. He couldn't think of a diversion.

Himey arrived, fully clothed, on the patio, about five minutes later. He stated Megan had slid home safely. Himey looked worse for wear.

"You don't look so good, bub. She work you over?"

"Too much tequila last night, methinks."

"Or all that hot tub water you just swallowed."

Himey looked at Eloy and turned green. He almost vomited just thinking about it—all the nasty things in that water.

"What the hell's that hanging out in the garage?" Himey said as he handed Eloy a fresh drink.

Eloy laughed. "Isn't that what they do for committing treason, the fucking traitors? Hang 'em high? So I hung the double-crossing sum-bitches."

"It ain't the clubs betraying you, E," Himey said, still laughing. "It's you, and you're the one betraying the clubs. A good set of Wilsons don't deserve to be hit that bad. You should have hung yourself."

"Well, I wasn't in the mood to hang myself. Not right yet anyhow. Got to get even with Echard, so they drew the short straw."

"By the way, we have a tee time Saturday morning at eight o'clock. Me, you, and Johnny boy," said Himey.

John Echard came through the back door with a beer in his hand and found a chair on the patio. Eloy surmised he had stopped on the way and helped himself to a beer from Eloy's refrigerator.

"Okay, boys, time to pay," said John.

Eloy handed John the four twenty-dollar bills.

"Thanks, and when are you available for your next whooping?"

"Himey tells me at eight o'clock on Saturday. And don't forget to bring those twenties with you. I think they're homesick. By the way, how is Megan?"

Himey almost spit up his beer.

"She's awesome, E! She does yoga now and goes swimming three times a week. She is fit and trim and has the body of a twenty-year-old. Damn, is it firm!"

Behind John's back, a grinning Himey nodded yes.

"You know, guys, it's all I can do to keep her satisfied."

Himey shook his head no.

John saw him.

"What the hell you mean no?" he asked.

"We all think we satisfy them, but we don't. That's all."

"Well, maybe you guys, but not me. We do everything there is to do, damn near every night. So what's up with you and Cassie, Eloy? Rumor has it you two split."

"We were arguing about something stupid—me drinking, her PMSing."

Eloy raised the pitch of his voice. "She said, and I quote, 'You're still a goddamn caveman, aren't you? You still think you can grab us by the hair, drag us off to bed, fuck us, then go off hunting or playing golf and leave us to do everything else. And then when you finally come back around, you're a fucking drunk smart ass just looking for some fried meat and some pussy. You're incorrigible!'

"You know it was remarkable she described me so well, but I didn't say so considering the situation."

Eloy continued. "You know what, gents, I'm just a Neanderthal, and I damn sure enjoy being that way. Looking back on it, I could have and should have handled it better. But the problem is, PMS and scotch never have mixed too well."

Himey gave Eloy a thumbs-up sign saying he agreed, and then he spoke. "The only thing that goes well with PMS is nothing."

"The straw that finally broke the camel's back," Eloy said, "was a fight over how to eat an artichoke."

Himey started laughing so hard he almost choked on a sip of beer. "How the hell could you get into an argument over how to eat an artichoke? Do you even know how?"

"No, and therein was the problem. We went somewhere for dinner with those uppity-type flakes and all, and they served this whole artichoke. Now I know I'm a dumb ass, so I asked 'em, 'How do you eat one of these things?'

"Seems as though everyone at the table knew how 'cept me. I don't know where Cassie learned. One of the other women at the table tried to show me how to eat the damned thing. 'You peel off one of the leaves,' she said. 'Dip it in this sauce, and then kind of suck-bite the leaf and the tender part of the artichoke comes off.'

"I just looked at them dumbfounded. This same woman added that women who were good at eating artichokes were also better at oral sex. I told her I wouldn't know. I had never met anyone before who knew how to eat an artichoke, though I had been the recipient of several world-class blowjobs.

"She said, 'Surely, they must have known how.'

"The fight started when I asked the men at the table if it helped any of them any in sucking dicks. That's when, as Stan Buck says, the exit light came on and the tailgate went down."

"You know, I saw this saying about that, and damned if it ain't true," said Himey.

"What's that?" asked John.

"This gynecologist back in 1912. Hell, even back then they was having trouble. Anyway, this gynecologist, his name was something like Hermann Otto Kloepneckler."

"Who? Clop-neckler? You making this shit up?"

"No. Kloepneckler. He was an Austrian doctor of some sort. I'm not spoofin' you. He said, and you know I memorized this, 'The best engine in the world is a vagina. It can be started with one finger. It is self-lubricating. It takes any-sized piston. And it changes its own oil every four weeks. It is only a pity that the management system is so fucking temperamental.'"

Eloy laughed. "Explains it all, don't it?"

"There you go. Any chance for you two?"

Eloy looked at Himey and John and grinned. "Hell, I don't know."

Eloy paused for a long moment and then said, "Probably. I don't know. I would, but I don't know about her. I tell you, on the way home from Tennessee, driving all that way with no booze, thinking about all kinds of different things, you come to realize"—Eloy took a long drink of the scotch—"that the world sure looks way different through sober eyes."

"Well, E, think about this. Maybe Cassie likes her friends and what she does. The same way you like the Barbeque Circuit and all us guys. Ever think of that?"

Eloy sipped his drink and pondered the question.

"Considering what you just said, the relationship will never work. I'm not giving up the Barbeque Circuit," stated Eloy emphatically. The he added, "And there are plenty of other women to be had who can give me more trouble than I want."

"That might make a good song title," said John.

"What's that?"

"The world looks better through sober eyes."

Eloy removed his clubs from the hangman's noose, telling them that none other than the governor of Texas had called and personally pardoned them. He also told them they shouldn't get too cocky, because they could be convicted of other charges and he might just give them a burial at sea the next time. He told them that he might just put them down at the pawnshop next to them cheap-ass Kroydons and all of those Sam Sneed and Julius Boros sets from Sears and Ward's. He told them there were plenty of sets of clubs in the pro shop just itching to get outdoors, get some fresh air, and be subservient to a master. "Now quit your moaning and hit some quality shots for my broke-dick ass—or some MacGregor might be in my future."

He laughed out loud at himself. Dumb son of a bitch, talking to golf clubs like they were human.

Saturday at seven fifteen in the morning, Eloy walked into the Green Tree Country Club. He was greeted by the head professional, Moses Jenks.

"Morning, Eloy. I see you have the first tee time on the new North Course. Let me know how it plays."

Lights started flashing in Eloy's head. "No one else has ever played it?

"Nope."

"Course record?"

"Whatever you shoot."

"Good to know. Any advice on my swing?"

"Just hit it three quarters and you'll be fine. You're overswinging a bit."

Eloy met John and Himey on the driving range. He tried Moses's advice and hit the ball surprising well.

Eloy, Himey, and John were to be the first official group to play the new North Course. They made the same bets as they had the last time they played—twenty-dollar, two-down automatic, press bets.

Eloy didn't like press bets. How was it fair if you won four holes then lost two holes and you were even? He never figured it out. But he played the bet anyway. It was the only way John would bet.

Eloy offered another bet, for a hundred dollars, if John wanted it. Eloy would set the course record on the North Course.

John thought it was such a good bet that he enthusiastically doubled the bet to $200. It was an easy bet for Eloy. All he had to do was beat John and Himey. If needed, Himey would throw off and earn him a little parking-lot money.

Parking-lot money was when someone threw off on their game to help their buddy beat an opponent, or opponents, and then the winners would split the profits in the parking lot.

John was unaware they were the first official group to play the new North Course. John was dumb like that. Mark down two easy one-hundred-dollar bills for Eloy.

Neither Himey nor John knew that Eloy had walked the North Course the day before and had marked down some key yardages, especially where water was concerned.

On the first hole, a 408-yard par-four, Eloy hit his approach shot into the left greenside bunker. But he made an easy par with a great bunker shot.

The second hole was a 387-yard par-four with water guarding the right side of the fairway. John looked down the fairway and remarked, "Anyone got any idea how far that water is?"

"Two forty," said Eloy nonchalantly.

"Bullshit," said John immediately. "You don't know. You just said that to make me hit a layup. It's farther than that."

John selected his driver and proceeded to hit his tee shot into to water hazard.

Eloy grinned and then hit his three-wood short of the water. John shot Eloy a dirty look but didn't say anything.

The same thing happened on the 395-yard fourth hole, but this time John paid attention. "How do you know that?" asked John.

"I just got a knack for yardages, special gift," stated Eloy.

Himey and Eloy drove off in their golf carts.

When they were where John couldn't hear them, Himey said, "You walked it off didn't you?"

Eloy just grinned.

Eloy birdied the 208-yard par-three fifth hole. He played through the eighth hole with all pars.

He made a great save for par on the 455-yard eighth. Another great sand shot from the bunker behind the green.

He was one under par coming to the last hole of the North Course. It was a brute of a hole at 476 yards and into a stiff southwest wind.

Eloy hit his best tee ball of the day but still had 226 yards to the green. He hit his best three-wood and was just short and to the right of the green.

"Oughta make this a par-five," Himey said.

"No shit!" Eloy and John said in unison.

Eloy stroked his chip shot perfectly and watched it roll into the hole for a birdie three.

He beat John out of three bets and scored a thirty-four.

They played the West Course for their second nine. Echard lost again. But for him, it was five twenties plus the two hundred for the course record.

Eloy played well following Moses's advice about the three quarter swing.

Eloy made sure Moses was in the Men's Grill when he asked John for payment on the bet for setting the course record on the North Course. A score of thirty-four was no big deal when dealing with course records.

"John, you lose a hundred on the original, plus two hundred on the course record bet."

"No way, Jose. Thirty-fours don't set any course records," said John.

"Sure they do. Hey, Moses, what's the course record on the North Course?"

Moses looked up from eating his lunch. "What was the lowest score shot in your group this morning?"

"Eloy shot thirty-four, and he thinks he set a course record," answered John, laughing.

"Then that's the course record, Mr. Echard," replied Moses.

"How the hell can that be? Thirty-four ain't shit!" said John in a shrill voice.

"Well, Mr. Echard, it's like this. Your group was the first official group to play the North Course. So by legal definition, that makes the lowest score in the first group the course record. Oh, and watch your language here in the Mixed Grill if you will, please."

Moses then turned his attention back to his lunch.

John was pissed off. He looked at Eloy and said, "You knew that, didn't you, you son of a bitch?"

Eloy laughed. "Hell yeah, I knew it. You don't think I'd make some stupid bet like that if I knew better, do you?"

"Sorry bastard. I need some evens on that somehow. Just wait until Doc gets here."

John jumped up and left the table.

"Who in the fuck is Doc?" asked Himey.

"Who knows?"

There was a long moment of silence as they both finished eating their sandwiches.

Eloy finally spoke. "You know, Himey, we've got to quit doing stuff like what happened the other day."

"You mean drinking tequila or poppin' bimbos?"

"Bimbos."

"What are we supposed to do, E? Me and Budro were just sitting here on the porch minding our own business, waiting on you, and she comes waltzing in the house, takes off her blouse, and then comes out the door with no bra on, them titties all bare and all. They was just wiggling and flashing there. I'm surprised them boys playing number three didn't see her. Then one of 'em titties spoke to Budro and the other spoke to me. They said, 'So are you gonna suck us or what?' I mean, we didn't chase her down, but we weren't turning it down either. Hard to turn down when it's just slipped on ya like that and you don't even have to work hard for it—or make a promise you ain't gonna keep. Surprise pussy be so goooood!"

"What happened to Budro?"

"He blew early . . . both ways. But you know we just couldn't turn it down. It would have been un-American."

"Yeah, yeah, I know. I know what R.T. says. You don't turn nothing down 'cept little black boys and you turn them face down. But goddamn, that's awfully close to home."

"Bad habits are hard to break, aren't they?"

"Damn if they ain't. Especially when you like 'em!"

"What we gonna do then?"

"I don't know. I think I may just go to jacking off. Hell, that way it can be whoever I want it to be, any time I want it to be. If I need it tighter, I can tighten it. If I want it looser, I can loosen it. If I want a little strange, I can change hands. If I want it a little exotic, I can alternate strokes between hands or just use a different type of lotion. Or maybe get a fuzzy sock of some sort. It will always be with me, won't cost extra for rooms, or booze, or food. When I'm finished I don't have to buy nothing—flowers, clothes, jewelry, nothing. It'll never talk back to me or talk behind my back or slip off some afternoon when I'm hitting balls and fuck one of my friends. And the only-est time it will ever double-cross me is when it hits that occasional rat-hook. Don't you think a man could sit still for that?"

"Works for me," said Himey. He put his glass to his lips and drank down his entire beer. He tipped his glass toward Eloy. "You ready for another?"

"Naw, I'm out."

CHAPTER 2

Eloy sat on his patio, enjoying the late evening and meditating. His thoughts were random, unstable, flashing from one subject to another. Then it came to him.

Tequila

Tequila has a dark, sadistic lure, I would say.
The results I know, but I still drink it anyway.
Some say tequila is a whiskey, but it's a narcotic.
'Cause when I drink it, I tend to become psychotic.
I'm tired of waking in the morning, this pain in
    my head,
My stomach churning and wishing I was dead.
I can't drink as much now, be it the white or gold.
It's still just a potent and now I'm getting old.
Just to recover takes a full day of staying in bed.
I'm not drinking it again, many times this I've said.
It's not a question of manhood, or a question of
    pride.
It's just that sometimes, things we like must be set
    aside.
I'm retiring it undefeated; on a pedestal, let
    tequila sit,
'Cause of all the times tried, I've never beaten it yet.

So stand and join me in giving tequila a hand.
And claim it as the champion, toughest in all
    the land!

He would give the poem to Himey. After all, he was the inspiration.

Contrary to how it seemed, he was lonely. He missed Cassie. The song title John had mentioned had been rolling around in his brain. He grabbed his notebook, flipped to a blank page, and scratched out a rough draft.

As he poured himself another scotch, a smart-ass remark came to mind. *I'm so miserable, it's just like you were here!*

He dialed Cassie's phone and only got her answering machine. "Cassie, this is Mr. Stupid, cordial but repentant. As usual, I screwed up and blew it. I would like to make it up to you somehow. I want you to forgive me, and if you're up to it and want to, would you please call and tell me where and when to come groveling. I'll come humble and with bells on. By the way, think about this, if you will."

Eloy read her the song he had just finished.

Through Sober Eyes

I never knew what you meant to me,
Till the blindness left and I could see.
And Lord, the things I never knew
Till I woke up and was without you.
It's all clear to me and now I realize
The world looks different—through sober eyes.

I never knew I could be so blue,
Sitting here alone and without you.
And I'm sorry I drove us apart.
I sit here sad, with a broken heart.
So forgive me, please. I'm on my knees
And finally, I realize
The world looks different—through sober eyes.

With hope, he hung up the phone.

Eloy showered the next morning, poured some coffee, and returned to the patio. He dialed Billy Clyde Posey at the Clovis, New Mexico, municipal golf course.

In a low monotone draw, the phone was answered. "Clovis Municipal Golf Course. How may I assist you?"

"Billy Clyde, it's Eloy."

"Hey, pard, how you hanging?"

"I'm coming to play at Colonial Park this weekend. Got any time to take a look at me?"

"What'd you do, have plastic surgery or something?"

"No, honey, I meant my golf swing."

"Oh," said Billy Clyde, laughing at his own joke. "I got time. C'mon."

Eloy was playing with Bonner Bennet in the Eastern New Mexico Invitational at Colonial Park Country Club. It was a two-man best ball format, and most of the best players from eastern New Mexico and the panhandle of Texas were entered. It would require two days hard work if they were going to win this tournament.

Bennet was on the top of his game. Eloy wasn't.

Eloy arrived in Clovis on Thursday, checked into the Holiday Inn, and then drove to the municipal golf course to see Billy Clyde. Billy Clyde knew more about golf and how to play it than a rabbit did about running.

Eloy found him drinking coffee in the pro shop, with the usual cigarette dangling from his mouth.

"How ya doin', pard?" said Billy Clyde as he greeted Eloy, the cigarette never leaving his mouth.

"I'm starting to play better, BC. Got a little tip last week from Jenks and it's helped. Just need you to look at it and refine it."

"Okay, get some balls and go warm up. I'll be along in a minute," said Billy Clyde, blowing smoke out of his nose.

"I just want to make sure that in my trying to achieve perfection that I'm not simply reaching mediocrity. I do also know that if you only reach mediocrity then you're never worth shit at whatever you are trying to do."

Billy Clyde raised his eyebrows and gave Eloy a quizzical look. "That is pretty profound for someone who only thinks about golf, pussy, and booze."

Eloy laughed. "Well, BC, a random thought of unknown origin does pop into my mind sometimes before lunch, 'cause after lunch, golf is for the rest of the daylight hours, then women and whiskey are for nocturnal pursuits."

Billy Clyde laughed. His laughter caused the ashes from his cigarette, which had remained in this mouth during the whole conversation, to fall into his coffee cup. Billy Clyde took his last puff from the cigarette, blew the smoke out of his mouth this time, and then put the cigarette butt in the now spoiled coffee. "Let's go."

Billy Clyde watched Eloy hit balls for about thirty minutes.

Finally he spoke. "It looks really good, pard. One thing, try to brace it better with the left arm at the top. It's hard for anything to go wrong with that left arm braced properly, especially on the wedges."

Eloy hit a few more shots using Billy Clyde's advice.

Damn, he could hit the ball crisp. The ball exploded off his irons . . . Straight and high.

"Why didn't you tell me this before now?" asked Eloy with questioning in his voice.

"You didn't need this before. Since you hurt your back, your body can't respond to your old swing. This is the best way now with the bad back and all."

"Any other advice?"

"Try to roll your putts eight inches past the hole. Not six, not twelve. Eight. That'll get it done."

As they were walking back to the clubhouse, Eloy noticed the back of Billy Clyde's hair looked like it had been cut with a pair of pinking shears or a pair of those shears people used for trimming hedges. He couldn't help but laugh. "Clyde, where in the hell did you get that haircut?"

"Down at Edgar's funeral home. They give 'em out free on Mondays and Tuesdays. The trainees do 'em. Why? Doesn't it look good?"

"Well, you might want someone to clean up the back."

"Goddamn it. I knew there would be a problem when they had me lay down in that fucking casket."

Eloy took his refined swing to Colonial Park Country Club to give it a test. He saw three men about to tee off. One was the man who owned the store called The Hat Barn, one was a pharmaceutical salesman, and the other was a local homebuilder.

Some said the local homebuilder was also a pharmaceutical salesman, but not prescription drugs.

Eloy joined them, and they played six-hole robins to keep the game fair. In six-hole robins, three six-hole matches are played, two players against the other two. The players change partners after each six-hole match so that each player in the group partners every other player in the group.

Eloy's new swing didn't need too much testing. And neither did his putting. He was in awe of how good he hit the ball and how good he putted.

He was on the winning team in each of the six-hole robins.

When the eighteen holes ended, Eloy had shot a sixty-two, setting a new noncompetitive course record. He asked the men not to mention it to Bonner Bennet, so he wouldn't expect a score like that again during the tournament. It was happy hour and Eloy bribed the men with a couple of drinks.

Eloy left Colonial Park and went to find Ben Jaymen. He drove to the Mabry Lounge, went in the side door, and looked for Ben. But Ben wasn't there.

He was told Ben was at the Green Lantern Lounge.

Eloy left the Mabry without having a drink and drove to the Green Lantern Lounge in downtown Clovis. He entered and found

Ben sitting at one of the corner tables. Eloy thought it strange that he was sitting alone. Ben usually had somebody cornered—or vice versa.

Ben saw Eloy as he came in the door. "Hey, E, what you know for the good of the world?" said Ben, motioning for Eloy to join him.

"I only know one thing that's for certain: worms can't fall down."

Ben looked at Eloy with this strange look. He thought anyone who could or would think of things like that just didn't have enough going on upstairs, or had too much time on their hands. Then again, maybe chemicals had done gone and ruined Eloy's mind. Or he landed on his head during one of those combat jumps.

"So what the hell you doing in here anyway, Benny J? Why aren't you over at your own place?"

"Hell, every time I try to have a good time at the Mabry, I'm either refereeing a fight or being a marriage consultant, or someone's always wanting me to buy all the drinks. It's cheaper on me to come here and drink and buy my own. But I would buy you one."

As Eloy was about to reply, there was a commotion at the bar. One of the regular customers, a fellow named Bull Ray, was causing a stir.

Bull Ray was a local talent that had gone to waste, another case of alcohol and pussy ruining a man's mind.

He was almost an exact double of Willie Nelson and could sing like him too. The only problem was that he couldn't stay sober enough to sing more than one set at a time. Bull Ray just liked alcohol more than he liked himself. They say he wasn't born—he was just squeezed out of a bartender's rag.

Bull Ray was sitting at the bar. He was leaning back on the barstool with his knees propped up on the edge of the bar. He was wearing some Levi's jeans he had cut off into shorts. The shorts were cut way too short—and he wasn't wearing any underwear. The problem was the shorts were so short that his dick was sticking out one of the legs and the head was exposed.

The woman tending bar pointed it out and told him he couldn't sit there like that. She said he couldn't wear those shorts in the Green Lantern anymore.

Bull Ray asked her, "So you don't want me to wear these shorts in here anymore?"

She told him no.

So Bull Ray went into the men's room, removed his shorts, and then returned to his bar stool. He was completely naked. "Now hon, does that work better for you?" he said as he sat down and drank his Budweiser.

Ben and Eloy sat and talked while the Clovis Police came and carried Bull Ray away.

"Did you hear Patricia bought the country club?"

"Really? Savings and loan must be doing well."

"Don't know. Rumor has it her daddy was loaded. Then right after he died, she made the purchase."

One of the girls in the corner booth got up and walked toward the restroom. It interrupted their conversation.

Her T-shirt read, BEST IF USED BY TOMORROW.

"Eloy, I'm thinking I'm gonna use her by then, along with those two good-looking things sitting over there in the corner."

"I think you're gonna need some help, is what I'm thinking."

Eloy awoke the next morning and didn't know where he was. Carefully, with only one eye open, he looked around and saw he was lying on a bed in some room. He looked to see if anyone else was in the room. He also checked to see if he was at someone's house and should to be vacating as soon as possible—or if he was in a motel somewhere. Slowly, he determined he was at the Holiday Inn.

He was lying face down across the king-size bed with only his slacks on. He didn't have on a shirt, or shoes, or socks. His head was hanging over the bed and he could see a towel embroidered with HOLIDAY INN lying on the floor.

He arose, slowly, looked around, and didn't see his shoes, socks, or shirt anywhere. His watch and rings weren't on his hands. He looked everywhere and couldn't find them. Panic was about set in.

He searched his memory and couldn't remember anything about last night past the episode where the police took Bull Ray to jail. He didn't remember leaving the Green Lantern, and he certainly didn't remember driving to the Holiday Inn.

He washed his face and tried to clear his head.

That's when he noticed that the door to the hotel room was open. *You know you are fairly well hung over when you don't notice at first glance your motel room door is wide open.*

That's when he saw one of his shoes in the doorway. As he picked up his shoe, the sight of his car caught his eye.

The driver's side door was open. He saw the other shoe by his car door.

Eloy tiptoed to the car, the gravel embedded in asphalt parking lot hurting his bare feet, and looked inside.

It was a miracle! There lay his shirt, his wallet, his watch, and his rings.

He quickly checked his wallet and found nothing missing.

There was no way to know how long they been exposed with the car door wide open. By all rights, he should have lost everything. It was remarkable no one had seen them and taken them.

It had to be a sign from the captain, an omen.

Eloy needed to straighten his ass up and start flying right. The captain was taking care of him, but he didn't know why. He almost had a religious experience—*almost.*

After a long, hot shower, one pot of strong black coffee, and two red beers, Eloy finally got his wits about him. He couldn't remember the last time he'd eaten, so he went to Cook's Truck Stop for breakfast.

He ate a big breakfast. Three eggs over easy, a hamburger steak cooked medium, french fries—not hash browns—and biscuits and gravy. He thought it amazing that he didn't have a hangover. He was a bit fuzzy, but he didn't have a headache and he just couldn't remember anything about the night before.

Eloy knew one thing: being drunk and hungover was not something you can train for. In sports, the more you trained, usually the better you became—the faster, longer you could run, or jump, or swim, or do whatever you were training for. You built up your endurance. But you couldn't train for hangovers. Nope, no matter how many times you got drunk and had a hangover, you could never get used to the bleary, red eyes and the pain. Pain so bad that sometimes even your hair hurt!

Eloy met Bonner Bennet at noon at Colonial Park to play a practice round.

Bonner was actually impressed with Eloy's new swing and his ball striking.

Eloy still didn't putt particularly well, but it was okay. A small case of "the whiskey yips," he called it.

They went to the Mabry Lounge for dinner. Brisket, pork ribs, and sausage with pickles and onions, washed down with a few beers.

It was an unusual evening at the Mabry Lounge . . . No fights and no visits from lusty women.

They were paired on Saturday, the first day of the tournament, with Roone Benson and Artis Hedges. Of course, Benson and Hedges wanted a side bet. Eloy declined. He said he didn't want to get caught up in just trying to beat one team.

As they walked away, one of them—he didn't know which one—called him a chicken shit.

Eloy played a good round of golf—good, but not great. He birdied the four par-fives and made par on all of the par-threes and fours. No bogies. A nice sixty-eight.

In an individual competition, it would have been a great round, but not in a two-man best-ball competition.

To a bystander, Bonner played the better round. He made six birdies but also four bogies. Worse score than Eloy, but it didn't *look* worse. Two of Bonner's birdies were on the same holes Eloy birdied.

When Eloy was at his best, he wasn't flashy. He simply drove it in the fairway, hit it on the green, and made a putt or two— simple golf.

Together, they scored a sixty-four and were surprised they were tied for first place.

When they handed in their scorecard, a man who owned a local car dealership walked up to Bonner and said, "Great round, Bennet. Keep it up tomorrow."

He didn't say a word to Eloy.

Sunday, they were paired in the next-to-last group. There were four teams tied with a score of sixty-four, so the tournament committee flipped a coin to see who would be paired with whom.

Eloy and Bonner were, again, paired with Benson and Hedges.

Eloy parked his golf cart behind Benson and Hedges' golf cart. He got out of the cart and walked around to the side of their cart, where Hedges was sitting. The both of them looked directly at Eloy.

"Bonner talked this chicken shit into a bet with you. Twenty a stroke okay?"

"How 'bout twenty dollar two-downs?"

"I hate fucking press bets. Take it or leave it."

"Got it," said Roone.

Eloy walked back to his cart and sat down.

Bonner said. "What was that all about? I didn't talk you into shit."

"Well, I figure they are the team to beat. If we're gonna win, we gotta beat 'em all. I think we can handle it, so I made the bet." Eloy's tone was one of irritation. "I mean, how bad can they beat us?"

Bonner could only surmise that Eloy played better when he had a burn working . . . when he was half-mad.

Anyway, he did that day. They both made six birdies, and none on the same hole. They both made a bogey or two, but none counted for their team.

For some reason, one Eloy never could figure out, the putting green on the eighteenth hole at Colonial Park Country Club was being shown on a giant-screen television, via closed circuit, in the clubhouse. He could only guess that Patricia was trying to have an upscale Bar-B-Que Circuit event. Show all the members how it should be done right.

He was only guessing. He made a mental note to ask Patricia when he saw her again.

The closed-circuit television crew was interviewing each group as they finished. Eloy got special attention, as he was a past champion at Colonial Park.

As they got out of their cart at the eighteenth green, a television crewmember grabbed Eloy by the arm and began to ask him questions. Both audio and video were being fed live back to the clubhouse.

It irritated Bonner that they didn't wait until they were finished with their round.

Bonner quickly walked to Eloy. "Hey, man, we're not finished yet. We've got putts to make. Eloy, quit being famous and go make that pig-fucker!"

Eloy's face and Bonner's comment were sent live to the clubhouse.

Some in the clubhouse laughed.

Some said they thought they saw Patricia smile.

Some spit up the chips and salsa they were nibbling on.

Some just spit up.

The tennis players and people fresh from church were grossly offended.

That episode ended live interviews on television forever on the Bar-B-Que Circuit.

Eloy's putt on the eighteenth green was for an eagle three. He missed the putt, but the resulting birdie gave them a sixty-two. It was good for a two-shot victory.

When they handed in their scorecard, the man who owned a local car dealership walked up to Bonner and said, "Great round Bennet. Congratulations."

He again didn't say a word to Eloy.

Bonner looked at Eloy. "What'd you do? Fuck his wife or something?"

Eloy thought, *Oh shit. Maybe that's where I was Thursday night.*

Before Eloy left Clovis, he needed to see Ben. He had to find out what had happened to them that night at the Green Lantern.

He didn't have to look very far, he found Ben standing next to the scoreboard and drinking a cold Budweiser.

Benny reached behind the scoreboard and magically produced a scotch and water.

Eloy loved Benny.

"Congrats, E. Got 'em again, huh?"

"Well, the locals say Bonner got 'em, I only caddied."

"Just like you always do for R.T., right?"

"There you go. Benny, I got to know. What the hell happened the other night at the Green Lantern? I woke up the next morning and couldn't remember a damn thing."

Ben took off his cap and started scratching his head. He said, "I was coming to find you to ask you the same thing! Right now, I'm wishing I was what I was before, when I wished what I am now."

"What's the last thing you remember?"

Ben thought for a moment, rubbing his chin. "We were at someone's house. For the life of me, I can't remember who or where. Maybe it was an apartment."

"It wasn't that car dealer's house, was it?"

"No . . . No, it wasn't, but I do remember you came out of a bedroom with a shotgun."

"*Shotgun?*"

"Yep. You held it on me and made me take a drink of this nasty-assed tasting wine. Then you gave me the gun and said, 'Hold it on me so I can take a drink!'"

Eloy said, "Wow! You know, Ben, I thought I was over doing shit like that."

Ben got this stern look on his face. "You know, E, the last thing I remember you saying was, 'Are you gonna trust me or your common sense?' Sober, you're about half-fucking crazy anyway. But when you get a snoot full, you go full fucking asylum!"

CHAPTER 3

Eloy left Ben and went into the Colonial Park Country Club pro shop to collect his winnings.

Billy Clyde was waiting for him. "Played good, huh? C'mon, I'll buy us a drink."

"I need to get on the road. I'd like to get back home as soon as I can."

"Ain't like you to refuse a drink. C'mon, pard, me and Bonner got a proposition for you."

Eloy followed Billy Clyde back to the bar and they sat down at the table with Bonner Bennet.

"So what's this deal you and Clyde have for me?"

"We have a match tomorrow with some of the Hereford and Friona boys at Friona Country Club. We need you to go with us."

"I need to get on back."

"What the hell for? What you got going? You can go anywhere you want, any time you want, do anything you want, and there isn't anything anyone can do about it."

Patricia Strong set a Dewar's and water in front of Eloy.

"Just like the wind," she said. "Maybe we should just call him The Breeze."

He looked up at her.

She shrugged her shoulders and said, "Nice round, E. Better swing than before."

He was surprised she had noticed. "What was up with the TV thing?"

"Bad mistake. I forgot you and Bonner were playing."

"You two fuckers," said Eloy, turning his attention to Bonner and Posey, "why do you need me?"

"You kidding? Look how you played today. C'mon, pard, it'll be fun. Plus we might just make us a buck or two."

Patricia sat down another Dewar's and water in front of Eloy. She sat down in the empty chair at their table. Before anyone could say anything, Patricia motioned to the bartender to bring them all another round.

"Oh," she said, "make it a Bombay Sapphire and tonic for me, double lime."

"You know you're sitting with a really wonderful guy and two motherfuckers," said Eloy, looking at Patricia.

"There you go!" replied Patricia.

Eloy was sound asleep when he was awakened by someone knocking on his hotel door. Sleepily and groggily, he stumbled to the door. Through the peephole, he could see it was a woman.

He made sure the safety latch was on, and then he stood to one side and opened the door. He almost fell over with shock.

It was Patricia Strong—in disguise. She had worn a wig and topcoat to keep from being recognized.

He quickly let her in the room. Eloy reminded her that she'd told him that she didn't do one-night stands anymore.

She roughly pushed him back onto the bed. She didn't reply. She was taught to be a lady—taught it wasn't polite to talk when her mouth was full.

Friona was one of many small Texas towns with only a nine-hole golf course. If you looked on a map of the panhandle of Texas, Highway 60 would pass through Friona when driving from Clovis, New Mexico, on the way to Hereford and then on to Amarillo, Texas. A writer once said that if you were to pass though Friona on a brisk day around four in the afternoon, you could feel the loneliness.

Friona Country Club was the only place in Parmer County that served alcohol, so it was not uncommon to see semi-trucks parked on the side of the road late in the afternoon, with the drivers inside having a cold beer—or cocktail of choice.

Eloy, Billy Clyde, and Bonner arrived at the Friona Country Club at ten o'clock in the morning, Texas time. The parking lot was already full of cars. It looked like they might be having a tournament of some kind.

There wasn't a tournament that Monday. All the cars belonged to those who showed up to gamble and drink beer that day. Eloy wondered how come these men could afford to not work on a Monday.

It was easy for him and Billy Clyde. And Bonner only pretended he worked. Besides, it was summer. How could you sell commercial heaters in the summer?

When Eloy remarked about it, he was told that most of the other men were farmers and ranchers or self-employed and worked whenever they damn well pleased. "Anyways," someone said, "what the hell is it to you?"

Eloy, Billy Clyde, and Bonner unloaded their golf bags. They walked around to the back of the pro shop, found two empty golf carts, and strapped on their bags.

Inside the bar, they found the men from Hereford and Friona attempting to make teams and bets.

When the three entered the bar, a man named Jim Tom held up his hands to get everyone's attention. "Gentlemen, and I use the term loosely, I got it figured out. I'm tired of always playing against you guys. Let's all just play Posey, Bennet, and Baines."

"Works for me," most the men in the room said. "How we gonna set the teams?"

Jim Tom responded, "Shoot, how many we got here on our side?" He counted the number of players. "Okay, we got twelve. To make things simple, we'll just do a twelve on three-wheel."

"How's that work?" someone asked.

"Like this," said Jim Tom. "Every three-man combo plays those three, and every two-man combo plays their two-man combos."

"I'll play, but you figure it out. Don't sound simple to me," one man said.

The rest of the group said, "Amen."

"You okay with that, Clyde?" asked Jim Tom.

Billy Clyde looked at Eloy and Bonner.

Bonner shrugged his shoulders, indicating it was okay with him.

Eloy said, "Might as well. Can't dance. But do you realize how many bets that is?"

Someone in the back yelled, "It's 286 each," and then the person meekly added, "I think."

Eloy grabbed a Big Chief tablet and started scribbling. After a couple of minutes, he stopped and said, "Jim Tom, your side has fifty-five three-man combos. So if every man wheels, that would be 660 bets each. Plus there are the two-man combos; each guy has eleven partners. Another 132 bets, three-ways."

"Good god almighty, Jim Tom. That's too many bets," said Posey.

"Okay, I'll be the only swing on the three-man teams. Fifty-five bets on the three-ways and all of the two-teams."

"That's a hell of a lot of bets. How much we making 'em for?"

Jim Tom said, "In that case, let's just do a dollar a stroke."

Before they went to tee off, Eloy handed the lady tending bar the Big Chief tablet. He had lined out all of the bets. He told her to put each player's name beside a number and he would do the rest.

Thankfully, she agreed to do it.

"You know, if you weren't so pretty, I'd just marry you," Eloy said, showcasing his best charming smile.

"Now that doesn't make sense, does it, Sandy?" said Posey.

"Well, see, I wouldn't want to deprive all of mankind from her luscious wares by taking her off the market!" Eloy remarked, and then he gave Sandy a wink.

Friona Country Club was a very short nine-hole golf course measuring less than three thousand yards. The first hole was listed on the scorecard at 260 yards. It played slightly downhill and on the hard, sun-baked ground most everyone could hit it far enough to be on the green with their drive—if they hit it decently straight.

There were two par-fives, and if you hit your drive solidly enough, you would have less than two hundred yards for your second shot on both of them.

Friona was an easy golf course if you hit it straight, but if you didn't, then there was plenty of trouble to be found.

There were three five-man groups. Eloy, Billy Clyde, and Bonner each played with a different group. They played a lot faster than most figured they would.

Eloy's group finished first.

Bonner was in the second group.

Billy Clyde was in the last group.

Eloy was sitting in his golf cart and drinking his first beer when Bonner finished the last hole. Bonner hit a nice bump and run wedge next to the hole and had a tap-in for a birdie.

Bonner approached Eloy sitting in the cart. "Did that help you any?"

"Birdies never hurt, but I already had one."

"Did you have a good day?"

"I did. There wasn't a ball-talker in the whole group."

"Ball-talker! I hate those fuckers."

"Yeah, you know those kind who talk to your ball on every shot. *Hook. Cut. Spin. Bite. Get legs. Get up.* That kind of shit talk. Don't know why they do it. The ball can't hear a damn thing. You know once you give it a good whack, it can't hear shit with all that ringing in its ears."

Bonner laughed. "I never did like someone else's mouth on my golf ball. Mouths on balls are reserved for other things."

Eloy laughed and said, "Amen."

"If you played half as good as you did yesterday, we might have made a nice check."

"Will five twos help you any?"

"Five twos?"

"Five twos, and an eagle on twelve and one bogey on two. I beat those four I was playing with out of one twenty. Good day already."

Bonner let out a long whistle. "Still got it going, huh?"

Eloy grinned and nodded.

Eloy and Bonner figured their two-man team's total score. Bonner made birdie on number two where Eloy made his only bogey. Their best ball score was a fifty-eight.

They were standing on the covered porch, beer in hand, as Billy Clyde approached the last green.

The ninth/eighteenth hole was listed as 320 yards. It played slightly uphill, but usually with a southwest wind. Since it played downwind, it played shorter than the listed yardage, plus the fairway normally was hard as a rock.

Billy Clyde found his tee ball in the right rough next to a tree.

Both Eloy and Bonner were unconcerned, as they had both made a birdie on the eighteenth hole.

Eloy was taking a sip of a Miller Lite as Billy Clyde addressed his ball, took an abbreviated backswing, and kind of chopped down on the back of the ball.

Intently, Eloy watched the ball as it took flight. He poked Bonner in the ribs. "Watch this shit," he said without taking his eyes from the ball.

Eloy knew of what he spoke. He had seen the exact same shot before. Billy Clyde had hit one just like it when he and Eloy had their epic match back in 1980.

Eloy and Bonner watched Billy Clyde's ball. It hit just short of the green, bounced hard off the hardscrabble fairway, hit the green, then suddenly put on the brakes, spun left, and went into the hole for an eagle two.

Bonner, in his slow Southern drawl said, "Son of a bitch! Son of a bitching two banger!"

Eloy said, "I don't know about you, but I think just made $187."

"How you figure?" said Bonner, giving Eloy a high five.

"One dollar on each of the fifty-five three-way bets, plus the one hundred and thirty two mans I got with BC."

It took almost an hour and half to get all the scores counted for the twelve-man team. Eloy, Bonner, and Billy Clyde had theirs figured in about five minutes.

Eloy and Bonner had the fifty-eight. Bonner and Billy Clyde had the worst score of the three, a fifty-nine. Eloy and Billy Clyde shot a fifty-seven.

Their three-man team had a fifty-five.

When it was all tallied, Eloy, Bonner, and Billy Clyde had won $2,100. The split the money so each made $700.

Eloy laughed. How the hell could that happen? Dollar a stroke and win $700.

The teams that shot eight under, sixty-four, were all pissed off. One of them suggested a nine-hole mad match.

Only six remained to play. So they played a three-on-six wheel with all combinations in play. The bets were upped to twenty dollars a shot.

One team walked off when Eloy chipped in for an eagle two on the first hole—and they didn't pay when they left.

That left three on three.

Eloy, Bonner, and Billy Clyde played even better on the mad match nine than they had earlier.

Billy Clyde said it was the beer.

Coming into the last hole, they were four shots ahead on the three-man team. They were four shots ahead of one two-man team and five shots ahead of the other two-man teams.

The best Eloy could figure, he was up $360. Billy Clyde and Bonner must be too, he surmised.

"We want to press to get even," said Jim Tom as he walked to the ninth tee.

"For the day or for this nine?" Bonner said as he swung his driver back and forth.

"This nine."

"All ya in?" said Posey.

All nodded in agreement.

Eloy, Bonner, and Billy Clyde won another $700 each.

As Eloy put his clubs in his car and the money in his "Sock," Billy Clyde said, "It's good to have you back playing good, son."

"It is your fault."

"I know. But I didn't want to say it out loud. 'Fraid I couldn't get my hat back on."

"See ya at the Ross," commented Bonner.

Eloy was at the Friona Allsup's convenience store getting gas and something to eat and drink for the drive back to Midland. In Eloy's opinion, the Allsup's chain of convenience stores, based out of Clovis, had the best deep-fried chimichangas to be had.

He was about to check out when a young woman walked into the door. She wore a T-shirt that said, I COME WITH INSTRUCTIONS.

As she walked past Eloy, he remarked, "I bet you don't need much instruction, do you?"

The woman took two steps past Eloy and then stopped and turned to face Eloy.

"No, not really. Actually, if I'm wearing really tight Wranglers like the ones I have on, I can just squiggle around in the car seat and get it done."

"Care to give me a demonstration?"

CHAPTER 4

When Eloy returned from Friona, he had hoped to find a message from Cassie. There wasn't one. He guessed it was really over. He felt remorse—and anger at himself.

Eloy met R.T. Deacon for lunch at the Mixed Grill at Green Tree County Club on Tuesday. John Echard was there sitting with a man neither one of them had seen before.

John called them over to their table.

"Eloy Baines, R.T. Deacon, this is Doc Willis. Doc, meet Eloy Baines and R.T. Deacon. Doc here is probably the best left-handed golfer in the state," said Echard matter-of-factually. "Not only that, he may be one of the best players in the state."

"Is that so?" said R.T. as he gave Doc a hard look.

R.T. rummaged back in his memory, thinking about all the state tournaments he had played in, and he had never heard of Doc Willis. "Hmmm, I play in all the state events. Must have missed him somewhere along the line. I don't recognize the name."

"I just moved to Fort Worth, from Utah," Doc quickly replied.

"Yeah," said Echard, "we're going to play the Hogan Park Partnership together. We'll be giving you two some competition."

"Sounds like fun to me," said Eloy.

"I've heard a lot about you. Are you playing tomorrow, Eloy?" asked Doc.

"No. R.T. has got me doing some kind of couples thing. But I thought John was going out of town tonight."

Echard said, "I am, but Doc's gonna stay and play and get a look at the course. I set it up with Moses."

"So you're pussin' out, are you? Gonna go play with the women?" said Doc, looking at Eloy with a smug grin on his face.

Eloy didn't know what Echard had told this Doc character. But Eloy didn't like the tone of Doc's voice and developed an instant dislike for the man. Eloy's mood turned hostile. "Call it what you want. What the fuck's it to you anyway?"

It had been a long time since he felt like hitting anyone in the nose, but the sensation came over him instantly—and he liked it.

"John said you cheap-shot him on a bet and I thought you might want some straight-up competition," replied Doc, and then he grinned again.

Echard's face flushed red.

Eloy started around the table for Doc but R.T. grabbed him.

Quickly, Echard stood up and stood in front of Doc.

R.T. whispered in Eloy's ear. "Little low life weasel ain't worth it, E. I don't want you whipping his ass in here."

"Why's that?" asked Eloy, struggling to get past R.T.

"Cause I'm gonna do it!" Then R.T. started toward Doc.

Echard quickly grabbed Doc and ushered him to the front door.

"Have you ever met a sum-bitch that would talk like that to a stranger?" said Eloy angrily.

"I bet when he was born his mama wouldn't even let him nurse," said R.T.

"Hell, whatever gave birth to him probably didn't even have tits. I'll tell you one thing. If I see the motherfucker out here tomorrow, I'm gonna put my wedge to use for something besides hitting goddamn shanks on seventeen."

"Did you see his teeth?" asked R.T.

Doc Willis, the one time he did grin, showed his stained teeth—his teeth looked almost green.

"Yeah, how would you like to kiss that sum-bitch? Fucking green-teeth cocksucker looks like he's been chewing too much tobacco or something."

"Yeah," said R.T. "Or just eatin' his own shit, green-teeth motherfucker."

Eloy started toward the front door.

"Where you going now?"

"I'm going to the parking lot and kick his ass, R.T. I don't care if they throw me outta here. I've been thrown in better. Anyway, I may have enough money to just buy this fucking joint."

R.T. grabbed Eloy by the arm just as he went out the front door. They saw Echard's car and what they assumed was Doc's car pulling out of the parking lot.

"Chicken shit fucker. I'm gonna get his ass somehow, R.T. I don't know, how but I am. Just like that guy in Augusta that time, remember when Dad and me went out there? Think I can't play. Fuck him."

"Yeah, I remember."

Dad and Eloy had gone to the Masters in Augusta, Georgia, in 1981. Dad and Eloy were invited to play golf at Augusta Country Club by Tom Kite Sr. Augusta Country Club lay adjacent to Augusta National Golf Club, where the Masters is played.

On that day, they were paired with a member, which was the only way a nonmember could play. On the first tee, the member asked them their handicaps. Tom Kite Sr. said he was a six, Dad said he was a sixteen, and Eloy told him he was a zero.

"Well, you won't be a zero here," the member said to Eloy in a smart-ass way.

It pissed Eloy off, but he was a guest, so what the hell? He didn't say anything. He was just going to play his ass off.

The member said since they were from West Texas, where there weren't any trees and such, that he would adjust their handicaps to account for all of the tall pines and narrow fairways they would encounter.

Eloy could only assume that this Augusta member had never seen Amarillo Country Club, Lubbock Country Club, or Midland

Country Club. Maybe you didn't call those trees because they weren't sixty feet tall.

The member was a six handicap himself, so he gave each of them four extra shots. Eloy was now a four, Dad a twenty, and Tom Kite Sr. a ten.

After the match was over, the member was last seen shaking his head and much lighter in the pocket book.

Dad remarked how much better a porterhouse tasted when it was purchased with someone else's money.

Eloy said, "You know, Dewar's is the same way."

Eloy went to the Green Tree Country Club driving range to work off his hostility. He hit a whole bucket of balls with his driver. He hit them as hard as he could. He felt better now.

Hogan Park Municipal Golf Course had twenty-seven holes. It winded in and through the scrub mesquites, which in themselves provided plenty of peril for a wayward golf shot.

R.T. pulled his car into the parking lot and immediately saw John Echard and Doc Willis on the driving range. He also saw Eloy on the very end, already beginning his warm-up routine.

R.T. put on his shoes, got his clubs, and joined Eloy on the driving range. "Did you see the Bobbsey Twins down there?"

"Piss on 'em," Eloy said with a hint of anger in his voice. "Ain't nothing but rodents. All rodents should be exterminated from golf courses."

Eloy went to the pro shop and saw the pairings. His anger level went up about ten points, but he remained calm. They were to play a sixsome with the Hogan Park Men's Golf Association champion, his partner, and Echard and Willis.

Eloy asked the head professional if he was mad at him or something for pairing him and R.T. in a sixsome.

"Had to put them somewhere. If I put them anywhere else, they would only slow down play. You guys play fast. Sorry."

When Eloy and R.T. got to the first tee, the other two teams were already there. Eloy walked up to the teeing area. He was cordial to both teams and introduced himself to the MGA champion and his partner. He reached into his right front pocket, removed a roll of money bound by a rubber band, and threw it on the ground.

"Me and R.T. will play for any of it . . . or all of it." He looked straight at Doc when he said it.

"We're good," said the MGA champion.

"We'll try a five-dollar Nassau," said Doc.

R.T. laughed. "Hell, Doc, I wouldn't lace my shoes for five dollars."

"Pretty fucking bold for the best left-handed player in the state," said Eloy as he picked up his roll of money.

On one of the par-four holes, John hit a poor shot and threw his iron in disgust. It almost hit Eloy. Eloy jumped out of the way of the flying missile just in time. Then he picked up John's club and threw it in the lake on the left side of the fairway.

John stared at Eloy in disbelief.

Willis used a ball retriever and pulled the club from the water.

After they completed their first nine holes, the MGA champion walked over to Eloy, pointed his thumb toward Willis, and said, "If that boy is the best left-handed golfer in this state, then I'm a Japanese airline pilot."

"Ah-so," said R.T.

At the end of the first day, Eloy and R.T. were tied with the MGA champion and his partner.

The Hogan Park Partnership probably didn't really qualify as a true Bar-B-Que Circuit event. They didn't have a Calcutta accompanied by any kind of dinner, let alone barbeque.

R.T. and Eloy decided to go to The Bar in downtown Midland for their evening frolics. They would invite Himey, Dad, and Budro.

Eloy left another message for Cassie. He was still trying but was concerned she wasn't.

They got a big table. R.T. and Kathy Wahl, Dad and Silvia, Ellis Budde and his wife, and Eloy were all seated when Himey arrived. He was accompanied by a woman no one recognized.

Eloy turned in his chair and saw that she was very pretty. He would have noticed her very fine body, but his eyes couldn't leave her face. It was her eyes. She had wonderful eyes. Push-me-down eyes. Don't-ever-close-your-eyes-to-kiss-me eyes. Don't-ever-close-your-eyes-to-make-love-to-me eyes.

Eloy was speechless. He immediately rose from his chair.

Eloy finally noticed her well-built body. She had a T-shirt on, and it read, HUNGRY, just above her mountainous tits. Her tits were big enough to stretch the corners of the H and the Y. Written across the stomach area was, I'VE GOT MILK.

The woman extended her hand and said, "Hi, my name is Dallas."

Eloy responded, "Nice name, Dallas. I'm E.B. Breeze."

Eloy thought he could detect her accent as being Cajun. He'd bet even money she was from New Orleans.

"Dallas, his real name is Eloy Baines. He's the best friend I've been telling you about. Eloy, this is Dallas Central, the NBA champion of the world."

Dallas quickly corrected Himey. "He always pronounces my name wrong. It's not *Central*. It is *Syn-trele*. Besides, he said his name was E.B. Breeze."

"It's just him. He gives everyone an alias in case he was to commit some deviant act."

"No wonder ya'll are good friends."

Eloy backed away from Dallas and took a good long look.

One thing, even as perfect as she was: she wouldn't make the top three in The Best Tits in Texas contest. Those still belonged to Cheryl Gail, Cassie, and RV Darlene. But hell, why be picky? He decided, right on the spot, there was now going to be a top five Best Tits in Texas. Finding the fifth one would be fun.

He later told Himey about it. Himey said, "What's wrong with the top ten?"

She must be missing something upstairs, thought Eloy. Something this good looking couldn't have enough sense to know if she was washing or hanging out. A case in point, he figured, was that she was dating Himey. He wondered how much money Himey had told her he had. He had probably told her he was a senator or something. Women like this just didn't date any-old-body.

She commented, in that Cajun, singsong voice, "Well, my goodness, Eloy Baines, in person. Everything I ever heard 'bout you, I thought maybe you could walk on wah-ta."

"Only late in the evening, given the proper blood alcohol level. Water, hot coals, hell, sometimes I can even fly!"

Eloy knew exactly what Himey meant when he said she was the NBA champion. He meant the National Bedroom Acrobatics champion.

"So what do you do for a living, besides make Himey here happy?"

"I'm a florist, you now, one of those people that say it with flowers."

Eloy couldn't help himself. "Got a bouquet that says, 'I'd like to have sex with you'?"

"Oh yesss, we do," she said, never missing a beat. "Himey has already purchased one. It's usually red and white and green."

"Red and white roses?"

"Oh nooooo. No no. Flowers just won't do in that situation. Nooooo, it is rubies and diamonds accompanied by an arrangement of several fresh, crisp, one-hundred-dollar bills."

"So are you two martini genies gonna order us an appetizer?" Kathy Wahl said, addressing R.T. and Eloy.

"Tell me, Kathy," said Sylvia, "what is a martini genie? I haven't heard that before."

Kathy grinned. "Just open a bottle and *poof!* There appears R.T. and Eloy."

She took R.T.'s arm and said, "Do you two realize you're concomitants?"

Eloy looked at her and said, "We're not communist. That's bullshit."

"I didn't say 'communist.' I said 'concomitants.'"

"So what's the difference?"

"A concomitant is something that accompanies or is collaterally connected to something else. Everywhere you guys go, there the others are. Do you know when you two are together that neither one of you is worth a shit?"

"Does that mean we're okay if we're apart?" inquired R.T.

Kathy rolled her eyes but didn't answer.

They were all enjoying drink and conversation when it happened.

Two stunners walked through the front door of The Bar. You could smell them before you could see them.

When Eloy first caught sight of them, he said, "Chick Filet's."

As they approached the bar area, the accompanying aroma from their bodies mesmerized everyone. It was one of those musky aromas. If you could have seen it, it would have spelled **SEX**, capital letters, bold print. It was an aroma made of the female pheromone mixed with a combination of perfect oils and perfumes.

With each step, each swish of their hips, an aromatic pleasure was sent everyone's way.

When the aroma made its way to the nasal passage of an unsuspecting male, it would cause his eyes to roll back, the short middle appendage below his waist to twitch, and perhaps his foot to uncontrollably tap the floor. If the unsuspecting male were sitting, he would squirm in his seat and perhaps put both hands in his lap like he had a pain in his groin. If he were standing, he would need to grab onto something to keep from falling down until the strength came back to his knees.

One of Himey's friends, a highway patrol narcotics agent, coined a name for it. He called it being "smell-fucked." He said it was a smell that just made you feel good all over. He said it must be what heaven smells like. Just the smell could cure what ailed a man.

Someone else said there were other aromas that made you feel good all over too. Like fresh bread baking, or an apple pie cooling on the table, or the smoky apple wood smell of pork brisket and ribs cooking.

The narcotics agent said those were in fact good smells, but he had never got a chubby smelling bread or pork ribs cooking.

"I guess that says it all," someone remarked.

Anyway, that was exactly what the two stunners did to the whole room—they smell-fucked them. It must have been extra good, because Silvia, the conservative one, remarked, "Mmmm . . . Delicious!"

One wore a low-cut blouse that gave everyone enough of a look to keep them speechless for a moment or two. And you could see the impression of her nipples on her blouse—luscious nipples.

"Ten-pointers," Eloy said. "The Chick Filet has nice tits, probably be USDA Choice."

"They're fake," replied Kathy. "Do you know what they call her cleavage?"

Neither one answered.

"The Silicon Valley," Kathy said, giving them a sly grin.

"I don't care. Do you care, R.T.?"

R.T. would have answered, but it might have made Kathy mad so he sat in silence. But he did shake his head in agreement.

Taking his eyes from the Chick Filet Eloy turned to Kathy. "You like Himey's new squeeze?"

Kathy looked over at Himey and Dallas. "Oh, you mean Dallas?"

"Yeah, she's kind of shiny, isn't she?" remarked R.T.

"Reckon she's got Mercedes pussy?" asked Eloy.

"She's not bad for a coon ass. You like her, don't you, E?" said Kathy.

Eloy nodded his head, denoting a yes answer.

"You have to remember what Dad says. No matter how good she looks, there is some ex-boyfriend or husband out there who is probably sick and tired of putting up with her shit. Why else would she be single?"

"Well, I wouldn't kick her outta bed for eatin' crackers."

"Just 'cause a chicken has wings doesn't mean it can fly."

There was a long pause. No one said anything. Then Kathy leaned close to Eloy and whispered, "Want to know what her pussy tastes like?"

Both R.T. and Eloy looked at Kathy with total surprise.

Eloy said, "I don't know about R.T., but I'm in!"

Kathy smiled and then, in a move that surprised both of them, leaned over and gave Eloy a great big kiss.

"There you go," she said.

Kathy and R.T. finished their drinks and left.

It took that amount of time for Eloy to recover from the kiss—and being completely surprised.

After he recovered, Eloy left the table and made his way to a barstool beside the Chick-Filet number one.

Lines from an old poem of his came to mind. He added some more. "Twinkle of ice in the glass, hand upon my knee, it came from the woman sitting next to me. So what would this evening hold, good things coming my way, senses already sated, by sight and smell, my, oh my, what a wonderful day."

When he sat down beside the Chick Filet he noticed the bartender's T-shirt. On it was printed, NOT A CADILLAC—BUT STILL A GOOD RIDE!

> Premium scotch . . . aged Angus beef . . . best friends
>   all around.
> Cozy atmosphere . . . pleasant talk . . . band blowing
>   good sound.
> I sat content . . . enjoying life . . . What else could I
>   ask for?
> Then the numbing aroma encased me . . . when they
>   walked in the door.
> One gorgeous, both built for pleasure, they sat at the
>   bar . . . waiting.
> Long legs, high heels, skirts short and tight, luscious
>   lips . . . baiting.

The hook was set, deep, the scent the lure . . .
   drawing me near.
Regret, maybe, but later . . . no consequences now . . .
   no fear.
What was worse . . . What could happen? Mortal sin?
Then I thought, *Oh god almighty . . . What if they
   are men?*

Eloy paid the bar tab and rose to leave with the two Chick Filet's. The bartender in the Cadillac T-shirt looked at the three and said, "Can I go with you?"

Eloy said, "What time do you get off?"

"Now," she said, "if I'm in."

Sunday at noon, R.T. pulled his car into the parking lot at the Hogan Park Municipal Golf Course. He spotted Eloy leaning against the hood of his car, drinking from a Styrofoam cup.

Surprisingly, Eloy thought, he wasn't tired as he thought he would be. He felt good, real good for being up half the night sipping on scotch and enduring a tag-team match from the stunners.

R.T. approached him and said, "What ya drinking?"

"Aiming juice," said Eloy handing the Styrofoam cup to R.T.

R.T. took the Styrofoam cup from Eloy and took a drink. It was a red beer, an ice-cold red beer.

"You know, I'm just guessing, but I bet you make contact with the Chick-Filet. Did she give up the cookie?" inquired R.T.

"Milk and cookie!" said Eloy, "but it was Chick Filet's, two not one. Plus the bartender."

Eloy opened the trunk of the Mercedes and made each of them a fresh, ice-cold red beer. Then they walked to the driving range.

Eloy slipped a solid white Foot Joy golf glove onto his left hand. He grabbed his 1976 Wilson Staff, Billy Casper special-grind pitching wedge and took a few practice swings.

"Janie too?" R.T. said with disbelief in his voice.

"Yep, she was interested only in the Filets, not me. But that's a great body behind those T-shirts. If it had not been for her providing the occasional diversion, I might not have survived."

"Tag team, are you too tired to play?"

"Nah, I'm good."

"Did you practice safe sex?"

"Nope, gave 'em my real name."

"And their names?"

"One of them was named Adie. The other was Oh Jesus . . . Or something like that. It was the only name I heard. You should have heard her speak in tongues when I did the old bowling ball hold on her. Sounded like Afghan-Iranian or something."

"Bowling balled her? What the hell is that?"

Eloy hit his first pitching wedge about ten yards left of the hundred-yard sign. Maybe being a little tired would help him slow down his tempo.

"You know, when you're doing your best tongue work on that little love button and you put your thumb in the honey hole and your finger in her ass. Hold her like a bowling ball. Makes 'em hump up like something hot hit 'em in the ass. They'll come faster than an orphan being called to dinner. And then that's when all of the foreign languages start."

"Son of a bitch, you fancy fucked 'em, didn't you?"

"Oh more than that. It was more like a tag-team Texas Death Match and multiple fancy fucks."

"Damn, Eloy, you should have called for help."

"I did, but you couldn't hear me. It was a bit muffled. So I made a hand and did my best and gave them the whole Pompeii, popsicle, missionary, dog, one-legged dog with a bone, saddle horn, reverse saddle horn, side saddle, both left and right, fold-over jackhammer, full-nelson, crossover, and scissor tailed. Wall, floor, shower, tub, kitchen—they need to buy some sturdier kitchen chairs. Even gave her a small sample of the who-dee-who-who-who yodel. It's in the blood, not preventable. I do's it all!"

"I bet it was fun, huh?"

"You know when we were kids and we could get a present for our birthday or for Christmas and we didn't know exactly what was inside and could only guess? Then we would tear off the bow and into the wrapping with great anticipation?'

R.T. shook his head yes.

"Well, that's the way it was!"

R.T. didn't know half of the positions Eloy had mentioned, but he was supposed to know so he didn't say anything. "By the way, you left out semi-dog style," he said. Then he hit a seven iron for his first warm-up shot.

"Nope, no semi-dog style. Did all of the sniffin' and lickin'. Hell, R.T., if you're gonna drive a race car, why go the speed limit?"

R.T. had to ask—his curiosity was piqued. "Pompeii, what the hell is that?"

"Well, you see, Ben thinks he invented fancy fucking, but he didn't. And I haven't ever wanted to burst his bubble, and you shouldn't either. Everyone needs to be famous for something, and for Ben it is fancy fucking. So don't tell him any difference. But he does get the credit for bringing it to West Texas. See, the ancient people of Pompeii invented and practiced every known sexual act and position there is or ever was. It was a decadent society. Ben probably had relatives there somewhere. I guess all that decadence pissed off God, 'cause he let loose that volcano and got 'em. It was the first documented case of someone actually having their ass smoked. It's a good thing we don't have volcanoes here."

"You know, I've been wondering . . . If Benny practices his sexual prowess he's so proud of, how come he's been married so many times? You know he married his last wife three different times. You'd think if he was fancy fucking her she would have stayed on, or so it seems."

"Hell, R.T., believe it or not, some women just don't go for all that stuff. Some are missionary style only, you know. She was one of those strange, missionary-only women, and he made it a lifetime project to convert her. But why he would have married her three times is beyond me. You would think he could have converted her without getting married. Anyway, you see what caused the trouble was the fact that the conversion didn't take and Benny kept practicing his fancy fucking—it just wasn't on her."

"I guess that explains it."

"There you go. By the way, tell Kathy it wasn't the Silicon Valley . . . It was Nature's Own."

"You know, E, you don't need to be led into temptation, you can find it all by yourself!"

Eloy played an excellent round of golf that day. His tiredness kept his tempo at a nice, slow pace. And his putting seemed extra sharp. *Maybe I've finally discovered the secret,* he mused.

They played again with the MGA champion and his partner. Eloy and R.T. played good, but the MGA champion and his partner played better—until the eighteenth hole.

The eighteenth hole was a slightly uphill, 205-yard par-three. R.T. and Eloy both found the green, but the champion and his partner missed wide to the right. R.T. and Eloy watched in amazement as both players hit their chip shots fat. Neither ball went more than five feet.

Then amazingly, they did it again. Their resulting double bogey gave R.T. and Eloy first place, but they didn't feel good about it.

They shook hands after the round.

The MGA champion put his putter in his bag. He then held his sand wedge up to his face and said, "Okay, you scooping sum-bitch, take this."

And then he began to slam the head of the club, violently, on the cart path. He slammed it again and again and again, each time saying, "You will never ever scoop on me again!" Each time he slammed it, his voice got louder and louder.

He beat the club on the cart path unmercifully until it was ruined, and then he viciously threw it against the golf cart, breaking it into two pieces.

"Damn, I feel better now!" he exclaimed.

The head of the broken club landed near Eloy and R.T. R.T. picked up the mangled club head and looked at the sole of the club.

The MGA champion had beaten it so severely that R.T. could barely make out the manufacturer's name stamped on the heel.

Eloy handed it back to its destructor. "I think it could use more bounce!"

They drove their golf cart to the veranda where the scores were being posted. Katy Wahl was there waiting for them. Eloy grabbed her around the waist and said, "Just between me you and a fence post, Miss Kathy . . . They were real!"

CHAPTER 5

Eloy got home, took a long hot shower, and then mixed a large dose of Macallan and checked his messages. There was only one.

It was from Cassie Channing.

It was the 'I know I should have called sooner' and 'we'll talk about it later' call. She made one remark that Eloy almost took the wrong way. But he was sure she was just trying to be cute. Had he been a little deeper into the Macallan, he might have misconstrued the meaning, but this time he only grinned. It was something that he had said one time.

Cassie said in her message, "I'm so miserable, it's just like you are here!"

The scotch and the call warmed Eloy and sent him into deep thoughts.

He was brought back to reality by the ringing of his telephone. He wasn't sure who it was at this hour of the night. He was hoping it was Cassie again.

"Hello," he said.

"Eloy, this is Roone."

"What's up, Roone? Looking for some easy pickings?"

"Don't know any easy pickings. I did meet Slim Pickens once. Listen, I've committed to this tournament this coming weekend at Pine Hills. I was going to play with Artis, but he suddenly came up lame or got sick or something. I know you're a chicken shit, but I would like for you to take his place." Roone was laughing.

"So you want me to take Artis's place *this weekend?*"

"Yes, how about it?"

"What happened to Artis? Isn't like him to have anything else to do during the day. All of his extra circular activity is at night—late at night."

"I'll explain it when you get here. You coming?"

"I'm in."

After a few more scotches, Eloy recorded a new message on his answering machine. "Hello, this is E.B. Breeze. I am lost. I have gone to find myself. If you find me before I get back, please give me a drink and have me wait."

He decided to call his friend B.J. Lloyd Liljestrom in Lubbock.

B.J. was Himey Wilkinson's brother-in-law, married to Vanessa. B.J. and Eloy had played some tournaments together. B.J. wasn't as accomplished a player as Eloy or Bonner, but he was game and he wasn't afraid of anything.

It was with B.J. that Eloy had won his first Championship Flight tournament. At Plainview Country Club that particular Sunday, between the two, they hit it in the leather nine straight times.

Eloy once told Cassie that story and she didn't understand.

"'In the leather,' what's that?" she inquired.

"'In the leather' means that if the distance of your ball to the edge of the cup is less than the distance from the head of the putter to the bottom of the grip then it's called in the leather. That's why you see us measuring the putts. We put the head of the putter in the hole and then see if the ball is touching the grip or not. If it's between the head of the putter and the grip, then we say it's in the leather and it's good."

"Okay. But why do they call it 'in the leather'? All of the grips I have seen are rubber. Why don't they call it 'in the rubber'?"

"Damn, girl. You don't know anything, do you? In the olden days, before Lifesaver-flavored douches, all grips were made of leather. That's where the term comes from. And there are still a lot of putter grips, even today, made from leather. Actually, all of my clubs have leather grips. The rubber grip wasn't invented until a few years back when some guy, I think it was a guy in Dumas, slipped a dry condom over a slick, worn-out leather grip so he could hold on. Hell, I even think it was raining!"

"Yeah, you lie better than you tell the truth. No one has ever played golf with a dry condom for a grip."

"Don't be too damn sure. Have you ever been to Dumas?"

Eloy called B.J. He told him to set up a match with the locals, the ones who had beaten them out of some money back in the spring.

B.J. said that would be easy, as they had been looking for Eloy so they could score some easy cash.

Eloy told Himey he was going to Lubbock to play with B.J. Himey invited himself to go along. He said he would call Ben to meet him at Pine Hills.

During the drive to Lubbock, Eloy asked Himey how he met Dallas. Himey said he had met her at the florist shop, the new one over on Garfield Street. He went in to get some flowers for his mother; it was her birthday or something. He said when he first saw Dallas, she struck him so hard he started going back and buying flowers just so he could see her. Then one night he ran into her at the Hilton. He described the conversation.

> I said, "Dallas, I think we ought to go out sometime."
> She said, "That might be nice."
> I said, "Where would you like to go?"
> She said, "I don't know. What about you?"
> I said, "Pick your favorite place and I'll take you
>   there."

"You know me, Eloy. Hell, I would have taken her to Egypt if she would have said so and promised me the pussy."

> So she said, "I really don't have a favorite place. Do
>   you know of anything nice?"
> I said, "How about Mexico? You can have a really
>   good time there."
> She said, "Mexico? I don't know."

I said, "If you like sun, soft, sandy beaches, and
>   warm air, sitting at the pool drinking daiquiris,
>   being waited on hand and foot and having your
>   every whim being satisfied, eating the finest of
>   foods and shopping till you drop, and if you like
>   sex while being in a pretzel-like position, then
>   you will have a good time."
She said, "Oh my, all of that sounds just wonderful."

"So E, I'm grinning like a pig in slop and already got the phone
book out looking for a travel agent." Then she said, 'While you're
making the travel arrangements, could we get try out the pretzel
thing?' Hell, E, she moved from fifth place to first in a heartbeat."

"Yeah I can see where she would. When did you go to Mexico?"

"What the hell would I go there for?"

As Eloy pulled the red Mercedes convertible into the
Meadowbrook Municipal Golf Course parking lot the first person
he saw was B.J. Liljestrom. Eloy playfully tried to run him over.

B.J called himself "Bubba". He operated the Meadowbrook
Municipal Golf Course driving range.

Bubba always wore cut off Levi jeans shorts, ragged at the
bottoms, a golf shirt, and black and white saddle oxfords—no socks.

Even in the dead of winter when it was zero outside and the
wind was blowing a gale speed of fifty miles per hour you'd find
Bubba dressed the exact same way with the exception that he would
add an overcoat.

Every time he hit a real good tee ball or would make a putt you
could hear him exclaim, "Baby doll!"

Eloy asked him why the nickname Bubba.

Bubba told him his real name was Bolivar June and he didn't
take kind to being called Bolivar, and especially not June. It was the
only reason he could find to dislike his parents. Other than that,
they were okay.

"Why don't you just go by B.J. or Lloyd instead of Bubba?"
asked Eloy.

Bubba said B.J. Liljestrom sounded like some kind of shyster lawyer and Lloyd Liljestrom sounded even worse to him, or like a child molester or faggot or something, so Bubba was his choice. Anyway, he said, "Who the hell has four names for Pete's sake?"

Eloy parked his car.

Bubba picked him up in the golf cart and took him to the driving range.

Himey and Bubba bear-hugged like brothers would do.

B.J. stuck out his index finger and Eloy swiped it with his index finger. It was just B.J.'s way of shaking hands.

Eloy told Bubba that he and Himey had a new name for him, better than Bubba. "Your new name is now Monga, Monga Lloyd."

Bubba thought about it for a minute and then gave his permission. Bubba didn't seem too concerned that it might offend some people—Eloy wasn't concerned either.

Bubba always called Eloy EeeBee, which was short for the initials in Eloy's name: E.B.

Eloy mentioned to Bubba the name Patricia had given him: The Breeze.

Bubba said it was perfect: E.B. Breeze.

Bubba had arranged a gambling match with some Meadow Brook regulars: three black hustlers, one being Willie Hickey, the cart barn manager at Meadowbrook, another being Dancing D. Dan, whose feet never stopped moving even when he was hitting the ball, and Weldon the Hairdresser.

Eloy knew Willie and Dancing D. They were two of the ones who had bested Eloy and B.J. earlier in the spring.

"Who has us trapped today?" asked Eloy.

"Willie Hickey, Dancing D., and that spooky-looking fucker over there," said Bubba, pointing to the far end of the driving range.

Eloy scanned the people on the range and knew instantly who the person was.

At the far end of the range was a light-complexioned black man dressed in a purple and black matching short/shirt outfit. The shorts

were black with a purple V that started with the wide end at the hem
and ended in the point at the waist. The shirt had a matching V that
started with the small end at the waist and ended with the large end
at the shoulders.

Eloy had never seen an outfit like that even in the women's
department at Macy's or Dillard's or Latham's. The other odd thing
was the shirt had what appeared to be a cape on the back with
another matching V.

"What the fuck is that?" asked Eloy.

And then the man swung the golf club—crossed handed!

"What the fuck was that?" asked Eloy.

"That's Weldon. He's a little strange, little bit queer, goes both
ways I think, and he's a hair dresser. But don't be fooled. Sum-bitch
can play," answered Bubba with a little laugh in his voice. "You don't
mind playing with a black semi queer now, do you, EB?"

"You mean golf, right?"

"Oh, yeah, right."

"A little bit queer? You mean he only sucks little dicks just every
once in a while?"

Bubba laughed.

"What's with the cape? Does he think he can fly? He ain't got an
S on his chest, does he?" said Himey.

Bubba was laughing real hard by now.

"I'll play, but you're testing my racial limits, Monga. A black
queer hairdresser, what the fuck do you say if you lose? And by the
way, who's the seamstress?" countered Eloy.

"He is."

"Don't you mean in his case he's the tailor?"

"No, actually in his case, he is the seamstress!"

Eloy introduced himself to Weldon.

"Hi, I'm *Well-don*. I'm a hairdresser. How much you got in mind
losing today?" He spoke it with sort of a lisp. It was Weldon's way of
finding out if it was worth lacing up his golf shoes or not.

Well-don was almost too pretty to be a man, and even though he was black, his facial features didn't show it. His skin was extremely light for a black person.

His looks reminded Eloy a little bit of Little Richard.

Monga said he thought Weldon got up every morning and painted himself black just so he could be a minority and maybe get a little black pussy—or something—as a bonus.

Eloy and Bubba played all two-man combinations: Willie Hickey, Dancing D. Dan, and Weldon the Hairdresser. They threw in Himey on a three-way bet. No one wanted to give any strokes to Himey. The bets were to be ten-dollar, one-down automatics. If there was a zero working, then there would be no press.

"*Well-don*, be happy," Weldon the Hairdresser stated.

"Willie Hickey ain't jickey," stated the Meadowbrook Golf Course golf cart manager.

"My feets be dancing, man. My feets be dancing!" said Dancing D. Dan.

"It's show time," said Himey. "Talking is over."

Meadowbrook, in 1985, was a short but tight twenty-seven-hole golf course. On this particular day, they were going to play holes nineteen to twenty-seven first, the nine holes the locals called Squirrel Hollow, then play holes one to nine for their second nine.

The first hole on Squirrel Hollow was a downhill, 185-yard par-three. Eloy was the first to hit. He selected a five iron and made a smooth swing. The ball curved gently against the blue sky, hit the green, started rolling, and then found the hole. A hole-in-one!

"I'll be damned, son," said Eloy.

Bubba and Himey gave him a high five.

In unison, the three black opponents said, "Pre-ress your lucky white ass."

On the second hole, Bubba hit a great drive.

The he hit an eight iron for his second shot and it stopped three feet from the hole. He made the putt for a birdie.

"Pre-ress your lucky white ass," was heard again.

On the third hole of the Squirrel Hollow nine, a dogleg-left par-five with water in front and to the left side of the green, Bubba,

Himey, and Eloy hit good drives, long enough to go for the green on their second shots, hoping to make an eagle.

Bubba's second shot landed just short of the green, took a friendly hop, and stopped on the green about thirty feet from the hole.

Himey decided his lie was too risky to go for the green, so he played up short of the water.

Eloy's shot hooked too much and ended up to the left of the green, in the edge of the water hazard, with his ball immersed in about an inch of water.

Himey lofted a nice wedge to within six feet of the hole.

Eloy studied the situation only for a short time. He decided there was nothing to lose, since Bubba was on the green in two and Himey was close.

He took off one shoe, took his stance in the mud, careful not to touch the water with his sand wedge, and then swung down hard, making a huge splash.

When he looked up through the mud and water, he saw the ball land on the green and then gently wobble into the hole for an eagle.

Bubba and Himey picked up their balls and headed to the cart.

They heard as they drove off, "Pre-ress your lucky white ass!"

Bubba birdied the fourth hole.

Something magical was going on!

Eloy laughed. His laughing made their opponents mad.

"Pre-ress your lucky white ass!"

On the fifth hole, a par-four, Eloy hit an eight iron approach shot just behind the hole. It stopped momentarily, then the backspin took over and it spun backward into the hole. Another eagle!

Damn, thought Eloy, *Roone Benson must have jumped in my body.*

"What the fuck's going on here, E.B.?" asked Bubba in shock.

Himey was smiling.

Eloy could only shrug his shoulders. Then he quietly said, "I don't know about your team, but my team is giving them a good old country ass whipping."

Again, the press-bird was heard. "Pre-ress your lucky white ass! Lucky bitches."

Himey said, "Since these are automatics, why they keep saying that?"

They got into the cart and headed for the next tee.

Bubba said, "If we keep this up, we gonna own was some barbeque joints, a chitlins factory, and a shoeshine stand or two."

"Yeah," said Eloy, "we can manage, those but what the fuck we gonna do with a beauty shop?"

Both Eloy and Bubba continued to play good. Himey was playing okay, but with the scores Eloy and Bubba were making, he was only along for the ride.

They easily won all the bets on the first nine, and they didn't let up on the threesome on the second nine.

The fourth hole of the one-to-nine side, their thirteenth hole of the day, was a short par-five. Eloy hit his second shot into the bunker on the right side of the green. He hit his sand shot and it made a perfect splash, the kind when you hear it, you know it's a good shot.

And to everyone's surprise, it flew into the hole on the fly. Another eagle! From Meadowbrook Golf Course to downtown Lubbock at the Great Plains Building, you could hear Bubba yelling, "Baby Doll! Baby Doll! Baby fucking doll!"

Himey was smiling.

He yelled so loud it brought the assistant golf pro out to see what was going on.

Even louder, onlookers could hear, "Pre-ress your lucky white ass!" They were screaming the words.

Eloy told Bubba that he thought he saw Dancing Dan get a gun out of his bag.

Bubba replied, "Shoot me then, 'cause I'm in already in heaven."

Three holes later, Eloy did it again. On the last par-five of the day, he hit his second shot about fifty yards from the hole. He took out his sand wedge and made a slow, easy, swing. The ball rose off the face of the club, hit the green, spun a little left, and then disappeared into the hole.

Eloy looked up to the sky, waiting to be struck by lightning or something.

Bubba snapped his fingers five times. "Five fucking eagles—same fuckin' day. Five fucking eagles—same fucking day. Five fucking eagles. Write 'em down, Charlie Brown. This boy can play. Kick some of that black ass, E.B. Talk to me, sweet lips. Baby fucking doll! Baby fucking doll!"

Eloy looked straight at his three opponents, who were all in shock, puckered his lips, blew them a kiss, and said, "Kiss a pussy."

To add insult to injury, Bubba birdied the last hole with all the presses working.

The money they had lost in the spring was won back, plus much, much more. The amount was big enough that Willie Hickey and Weldon couldn't pay them all they lost. Dancing D. Dan paid what he lost. "Feets lost all their shoes," he said as he gave the money to Bubba.

"*Well-don,* will catch you-uns' later. Need to score some more looty."

Eloy could not help from asking, since he was on the upside of Weldon. "Tell me *Well-don*, I'm curious."

Weldon paused from his hasty exit. He didn't turn his body around, merely turned his head to look at Eloy and Bubba.

"Just what the hell is that fucking cape for anyway?"

A strange look came over Weldon's face. He said with some emotion in his voice, "It makes me be in-bin-cee-ble."

Bubba replied first. "Didn't seem to make you too invincible today, did it?"

"Eloy shit on me. He be white kryptonite, wedge-holin' bitch."

Willie Hickey said he wanted to play more. He wanted to play another nine holes—an emergency nine.

Eloy and Bubba hesitated.

"Looks," he said, "I needs another chance on evens. I gave you'uns a chance. Come on, man. I cain't be into losing them kind of Georges."

"Georges" was Willie's name for one-hundred-dollar bills.

They finally agreed to play what the locals called the Loop— the last three holes on the nine that was comprised of holes ten to eighteen. The loop consisted of an uphill par-four, a short downhill par-five, and then a sharp dogleg-right par-four. If you hit a tee ball hard and pure on the sharp dogleg-right par-four eighteenth, if you hit it extra high up and over a water tank with a little fade, and got the right bounce, you could drive the eighteenth green.

Legend had it Roone Benson had made a hole-in-one there.

On the first time around the Loop, Willie lost more money.

On the second time around the Loop, Willie lost to Bubba but broke even with Eloy and Himey.

On the third time around the Loop, Willie lost all bets again.

Himey told Willie the fourth time would be his and Bubba's last loop. They had promised Vanessa they would take her to her favorite place for dinner, The Fifty Yard Line Steak House.

Eloy said he could play until it got too dark to see.

Himey said, "No, Eloy is finished. He's part of the dinner party too."

Willie wanted to play for double or nothing for the whole day. Three holes medal play, no presses, low score wins.

"That's a hell of a lot of money, Willie. How you gonna pay if you lose?" asked Bubba.

Willie hit his tee ball up the right side of the sixteenth hole. "Just hush and hit," he said not answering Bubba's question.

Eloy told Bubba it was enough money and that Willie would choke anyway. When you were playing for more than you owned, it was damn hard not to freeze on a shot or two.

When they reached the eighteenth hole on that last loop, Willie was ahead of all three of them by one shot.

Willie stood on the tee of the dogleg-right par-four. He knew he could drive the green. He had a chance now to erase a very large debt he owed. He should have thought about the shot instead of the money.

He hesitated . . . He then swallowed the biggest choke bug ever swallowed.

He lined up at the water tower and swung extra hard. Willie hit the worst-looking duck hook ever seen by two white men playing with a black man. The ball went out about one hundred yards and then dove sharply left into a creek.

Eloy instantly thought that in all the years Meadowbrook had been in operation, that it was probably the first ball ever to take a bath in that part of the creek. One had to hit it *really bad* to put it where Willie My-Ass-Is-Now-Owned-By-Three-White-Men Hickey just had hit it.

Willie knew in an instant he had just lost more money than he had, and more than he might ever be able to pay. Hell, it was more than he made in a whole year. His eyes turned red. He almost cried.

He calmly walked to the cart, drew back his ill-bred, double-crossing, duck-hooking, burgundy-stained MacGregor driver, and slammed it into the V-shaped post that connects the top of the golf cart to the chassis.

The club wrapped itself around the post and snapped in half. The head of the club looked Willie in the eye, grinned an evil grin, and then came at him with such a force that when it hit him in the mouth, it knocked him to the ground.

Eloy and Bubba rushed over to see if he was okay. His mouth was bleeding. They looked and saw he had knocked out both of his front teeth.

Himey was laughing.

Eloy just couldn't help himself. He might get shot or he might get knifed, but he had to say it. "What did you do with all that money your mama gave you for smart lessons?"

Willie just held his mouth and didn't say anything. He was in severe pain with blood running down the side of his mouth.

"Goddamn, Willie, don't you know a feller can't eat oil-hardened persimmon?"

CHAPTER 6

Eloy pulled the red Mercedes convertible into the parking lot at the Pine Hills Golf Course on Saturday morning. He got out of the car and immediately saw Roone Benson on the wrong end of a shovel, the working end.

Eloy approached and spoke. "What's up, Roone? You ready?"

"I got to finished digging this ditch. Pro wants a new water line run to the barn."

"Are we still playing or you gonna have to work?"

"Don't worry about me. Just go figure out how to make some putts."

Eloy went to the driving range to get loose and hit a few balls. He greeted Himey and Ben, who were headed to the first tee.

When it was close to their tee time, Roone was still working on the wrong end of the shovel, digging the ditch. Eloy wondered why Roone didn't use a ditching machine.

When he asked, Roone told him, "Hell, E, I'm being paid by the hour. An hour here, an hour there, a man has to be somewhere making his money somehow. A ditching machine would just cut into my time."

"Well," said Eloy, "you could charge for both your time and the ditching machine's time and cost, and that way you could make twice as much per hour as you make now. You would do the job faster, make the same money or more, and then have more time to fleece the flock, or actually find another job."

Roone stared at Eloy for a moment and then said, "I knew there was a reason I asked you up here. I been hearing you were smart. Thought it was just bullshit the way you act sometimes."

Eloy got Roone's clubs from the back of his beat-up 1970 Chevrolet van and strapped them onto the rear of the golf cart. He drove around the maintenance building and relieved Roone of his manual labors, just as they were being called to the first tee. Roone had not hit a single practice shot or a practice putt. He didn't even have his golf shoes on.

Somehow, after the first eighteen holes, they had managed a sixty-six. The leaders had shot a sixty-four. The sixty-six didn't impress either Eloy or Roone. Hell, Roone had shot fifty-nine on his own ball three different times at Pine Hills. Eloy had witnessed one of them.

Over a beer in the clubhouse, Roone told Eloy what had happened to Artis. Artis wasn't really ill, but what happened to him did make him sick.

Artis and Bonner were playing some Texas Tech college boys at Meadowbrook Municipal Golf Course. The bets had gotten high this particular day. Artis hit his second shot on the par-five seventeenth and it lodged in the chain-link fence on the right side of the fairway.

The chain-link fence separated the Meadowbrook Golf Course from the adjacent street, Municipal Drive.

The college boys laughed at Artis, knowing there was no way he could hit the next shot. They knew he was going to lose the hole.

Artis knew it too, and he got mad—at them for laughing and at himself for hitting the ball there in the first place.

Artis went to his golf bag and got his gun. Artis always carried a gun in his golf bag. With the amount they played for, and who they sometimes played against, a man had to have a gun in his bag for protection. Sometimes, in some games, they would count the gun as one of their clubs. If they were playing USGA rules, the rules stated you could only carry fourteen clubs, which meant thirteen golf clubs and your gun. So the conversation would go, "Uh, how many guns you got in your bag, Leroy?"

"I gots two. A snub-nose .38 and a lil' .22 for capping shits like you," Leroy would say.

"Okay then," the other would say, "you got to lose your one and two iron."

Artis went to the ball lodged in the chain-link fence, pointed his snub-nose .38 at the ball, and shot it. *Bang!* Shot it right out of the fence. Part of the ball landed next to the green, and part of it landed in the street.

The college boys quit laughing.

Artis went up to the piece of the ball next to the green and shot it again. He looked at the college boys, grinned, and said, "That muthafuckin' piece was still alive."

Roone said a police car just happened to be passing by on Municipal Drive and part of the ball landed on the hood of the cruiser. They came and arrested Artis. It appeared that Artis also had some sort of parole violation. "Prison is a terrible place," said Roone. "Really not good if you are prone to not liking it up the old gazoo on occasion."

Eloy stayed at the Villa Inn on Fiftieth Street and Avenue Q in Lubbock. It was his favorite motel in Lubbock. He always got the suite with the upstairs bedroom.

The bar at the Villa Inn was on the second floor above the motel lobby and was one of the best bars in Lubbock. It always had good music and the food wasn't bad. Eloy invited Ben, Himey, Bubba and Vanessa to join him for the evening.

Friday nights at the Villa Inn were always the busiest. Most of the residents who came on Fridays were looking for love. That way, they had the whole weekend to learn to hate each other and not create a lasting relationship.

Saturday nights were a little tamer, and it was easier to dance if one were so inclined. The band didn't have to play so loud and could actually be heard over the conversations.

Eloy chose a large table and was enjoying his first scotch when the others arrived.

Vanessa gave Eloy a warm hug. "I hope you don't mind. I invited a couple of more people."

"No problem," Eloy said. "The more the merrier."

Eloy greeted Himey and Bubba. "Himey, Monga, glad you came."

"Monga?" quizzed Vanessa.

"It's Bubba's new nickname."

"So I can only assume that Eloy came up with that. And you agreed?" she said with that squint-eyed look showing her disapproval.

Bubbaa didn't say anything.

"You should both be ashamed."

Eloy grinned and shrugged his shoulders.

Then *bam!* The aroma hit Eloy and Himey at the same time.

They didn't need to see who it was. They knew.

It was the Chick-Filet.

The smell was the same as it had been at The Bar. And it had the same effect. *Smell-fuck.*

Eloy stood and turned around.

There she was, the Chick Filet named Adie.

The look on Eloy's face and on Adie's face was the same— complete surprise!

But she wasn't alone. She was being escorted—and not by another woman.

Vanessa rose from her chair and warmly hugged Adie and her escort.

Eloy stood and spoke. "Good gawd almighty, Jimmy Connors!" He extended his hand to Adie's escort.

"You know each other?" asked Vanessa with complete surprise in her voice.

Jimmy Connors spoke. "Why, heck yeah. Eloy and I grew up in the same neighborhood. Eloy, this is my wife, Adie."

Adie gave her hand to Eloy, kissed him lightly on the cheek, and said, "It's good to meet you. I've heard a lot about you from B.J."

"I hope it was all good. And you'll excuse me, but I have to say, my, oh my, you really smell good."

"Well, thank you. Oh, actually it was real good, I would say."

Eloy knew her meaning.

"She does smell wonderful, doesn't she? It's her own concoction," Jimmy said.

Vanessa continued the introductions.

"Adie, Jimmy, this is my brother, the one everyone calls Himey. His real name is James."

Himey rose from his chair and shook hands with them both.

"You've made quite a name for yourself, haven't you, Jimmy, becoming a House of Representatives member?" said Eloy.

"He is a blessed man," spoke Adie.

"Yes, he is."

Just as they all sat down, they were smell-fucked again.

Eloy turned his head and looked toward the door. Ben walked in the door and toward their table.

The woman with him was Oh Jesus.

That's what Eloy and Himey both said under their breath: "Oh Jesus!"

Jimmy Connors rose from his chair. "Gentlemen, meet my sister, Jamie. Do you remember her, Eloy?"

Eloy almost passed out. Jamie was only six years old when he and Jimmy graduated high school. He did remember her, but he didn't recognize her—though vaguely he remembered the red hair.

"Jamie, do you remember Eloy?"

Jamie took Eloy's hand. "Oh, I don't know how I could ever forget Eloy!"

Their tee time for Sunday day was at 2:00 p.m. The hard thing about being out of town and having to wait until 2:00 p.m. to play golf was finding something to do on a Sunday morning.

A lot of times in the past, Eloy would use the time getting rid of who ever had stayed over the night before, but that wasn't the case this Sunday.

It would have been perfect if he could have occupied his time with Adie and Jamie Oh Jesus. A guy can only chip and putt for so long in his motel room.

Eloy pulled into the Pine Hills parking lot at 12:30 p.m. and, just like the day before, he saw Roone digging on that ditch.

Roone saw Eloy and remarked the ditch-digger rental place wasn't open on Sundays.

Eloy figured that even at a moderate price, the water line to the barn was going to be pretty expensive.

Just as it was the day before, when it was time for their tee time, Roone was still digging the ditch. The same as the day before, Eloy got Roone's clubs and loaded them on the golf cart.

Again, Roone had not hit a single practice shot or a single practice putt.

"Roone, you don't seem too interested in this. You want to stay here and dig that ditch and let me just play 'em by myself?"

Roone looked hard at Eloy. "Oh, don't get a fucking burn working. Hell, I beat these guys all the time. Tell you what, you play like I know you can, keep us close, and I'll have that ditch out of my system by the back nine."

Eloy played good enough, with one assist from Roone, to keep them within two shots after the first nine holes were completed. And true to his word, Roone took care of the back nine.

He got a couple of beers, drank them down, popped his knuckles, and pronounced he was now ready.

The tenth hole at Pine Hills was a short downhill par-four. Roone hit his tee ball to the front edge of the green and then made the putt for an eagle two.

That eagle was just the beginning. Roone shot a six-under-par twenty-nine on the back nine.

Eloy helped him two shots for a team score of twenty-seven. They won by four shots.

When they were picking up their merchandise for first place, Eloy told Roone, "That was one hell of a nine holes, especially for a common ditch digger."

"Remember what R.T. told you, Eloy," replied Roone, carrying six dozen Titleist balls out the door. "Golf ain't all that hard if you don't panic."

A real funny thing happened to Ben at Pine Hills.

Eloy could only guess that he ate something bad that morning for breakfast, or maybe it was too much Oh Jesus. Either way, he got sick.

After Eloy put his merchandise in his car, he went to watch Ben and Himey. He grabbed some more beer and found them on the par-three seventeenth.

It was a good thing the eighteenth hole was their last.

Ben teed up his ball and swung. It was an unusually bad swing, even for Ben, and then he stood there for a few seconds, posing. An expression that was hard to describe came to his face.

Then this large explosion came from his ass.

He turned to Eloy and Himey and gave them a big grin like he was really proud of what had just come out of his ass—then the grin turned into a grimace.

Eloy saw this brown liquid running down Ben's leg. It was a vile, semi thick, foul-smelling liquid.

The poor boy had just shit his pants.

The situation was worsened due to the fact Ben was wearing white shorts and white socks.

Before he could get behind a bush to hide, the vile, semi thick, foul-smelling liquid found his socks and turned them brown. He rushed behind a bush and cleaned himself up the best he could, but he had to throw away his socks and underwear.

He finished the tournament with a towel tied around his waist to hide the massive shit stain on his shorts.

Himey, after he finally caught his breath from laughing so hard, remarked to Eloy, "Now that's the shits—ain't it?—when something like that is the highlight of your weekend."

"There you go."

CHAPTER 7

Spook, Bonner, and Benny Jaymen all showed up at Eloy's at the same time, on Tuesday the week of the Green Tree Country Club Member-Guest, The Jamboree.

It was Eloy's birthday week. Why celebrate only one day when you could celebrate a whole week, or even a month for that manner?

Eloy called Himey at Dallas's house. "Hey, bub, what's happening? How's Central Dallas?"

"I just finished playing the front side."

"That's good. The boys are here. What time do you want to play real golf?"

Dallas Syntrele, nude and still glistening from her front side having been played, slowly rolled onto her side, and then gently rolled onto her stomach.

"Eloy I don't have time for that shit. I just got permission to tee off on the back nine."

With that, Himey hung up the phone.

It's funny how golf and sex have the same terms, thought Eloy.

Eloy and guests went to join R.T. at the Green Tree Country Club Men's Grill.

R.T. called Eloy aside and told him about Doc Willis, Echard's friend. R.T. told him he had inquired among his contacts in Dallas and Fort Worth. Doc Willis's real name is Percy and he was a phony. He was not a doctor of anything. Doc is just a moniker for some reason. Some said he took it after Doc Holiday, but he doesn't have the nerves of steel that Holiday had. Decent player but never won anything that amounted to anything. He damn sure wasn't one of the best players in the state. He's wasn't even the best left-handed player in the state. Hell, he wasn't even the best left-handed player in Dallas or Fort Worth. For that matter, not even the best left-hander in Midland; Himey could beat him. All thunder, no lightning. If he were bacon, he wouldn't sizzle. He'd rather cheat you out of it than get if for free. At best, Doc was a seven handicap.

It must have been fate; at that moment, Doc and Echard came walking into the Men's Grill.

Eloy waited for them to approach. He noticed Doc slowed his pace and got one step behind Echard.

Percy Fucking Green Teeth Willis, chicken shit, seven-sided son of a bitch, thought Eloy.

R.T. went on alert, sensing Eloy's hostility.

"Johnny boy, just the man I've been looking for. Bonner and me are looking for someone to play our practice round with. You two available?"

"Yeah, we were coming to look for you. Where's Himey?"

"He's tied up, can't make it today."

"What's the matter? Is he playing in some couples event or something?" said Doc with his standard shit-smirk smile.

"He's just ducking you, Doc. Doesn't want to get roughed up in front of the home crowd!" exclaimed Echard.

"Ain't the case," Eloy replied angrily. "Himey's got no reason to duck some cocksucker like Doc. Now Doc might want to duck Himey if he keeps that lip running. Besides, John, I'm all this smart-assed motherfucker can handle today. Name your price, button the lip, and get on the first tee."

Eloy went to the phone and called Himey again. He told him what R.T. had said about Doc and what had been said about him.

Himey told him to load his clubs; he would be there in fifteen minutes.

Eloy, Bonner, and Himey played Doc and Echard on that Tuesday afternoon. Eloy and Bonner played Doc and Echard, giving up no strokes. Eloy and Himey played Doc and Echard, with Himey getting two strokes a side to make the bet even, or so Echard thought.

Bonner and Himey played them the same way.

"Okay, Green Teeth," Eloy said, using his most menacing voice, "Today is pop-a-smart-ass-in-the-ass day. You've been wanting me. Now you've got me," said Eloy, pointing his driver at Doc.

"Just name it," said John, speaking for Doc.

It never occurred to John that Eloy's golf game was as good as ever. John was dumb like that.

"Johnny boy, just have him stand on his head and I'll play him for whatever falls out."

"Just make it the same as the other bets," said Doc. "It'll be easier to keep that way."

"Hell, Doc, I can add up hundreds as well as I can twenties," remarked Bonner.

The bets stayed at twenty dollars.

Eloy played Doc even, and he gave Echard his normal three strokes per nine holes.

Bonner played Doc even, and he only had to give Echard one shot a side.

Himey played Echard even and managed to negotiate, via John, two strokes per nine from Doc. Doc and Echard might as well have taken a torch and burned their money.

"John's a little stupid, isn't he?" said Bonner.

"It's like this: when you're dead, you're dead. You don't know it, but everyone else does. Being stupid is the same way. It's like Billy Clyde said that time about someone. John isn't smart enough to realize he's stupid."

The first hole set the tone for the day. Eloy's first putt came to rest about twelve inches from the hole. He started to pick it up.

"Wait a minute there," said Doc with that shit-eating grin on his face. "You got some work left. Better bring your whisk broom."

Eloy stood up, looked at Doc, and said, "What the hell do you mean? We always give putts that are in-the-leather in this game!"

"Some say you have trouble with the short ones. I just want to see the stroke."

Eloy tapped in the putt. He tapped in all of his putts that day.

But the statement Doc made on the first hole came back to haunt him and Echard. They saw Doc move his ball on two different occasions.

"Cheatin' little fucker, ain't he?" said Bonner.

"Doesn't make any difference. He could tee it up everywhere and still not be worth a shit!" responded Eloy.

The headlines could have read, Massacre at Little Big Horn Part Two—Native American Kills White Man Again.

They settled the bets in the Men's Grill.

"Best I can make it is we somehow, I don't know how, owe three hundred and sixty dollars," said John in disbelief.

"Make that four-twenty," said Eloy with a stern look on his face.

"How do you figure?" asked Doc.

"Well, you picked up that putt on seventeen and John was in his pocket. Since you didn't finish the hole, you lost another bet, three-ways. That's how."

"Goddamn, Eloy. That was in the leather!" exclaimed John.

"Weren't playing leather today, John. Remember what Green Teeth said on number one?" said Himey.

"Who?"

"Doc. You know, Green Teeth."

John looked closely at Percy.

Percy grinned.

John had an epiphany. He now realized what Himey meant. "He just meant he wanted to see it one time, not every time."

"Bullshit. You had lockjaw all day. We putted out on every hole. You lose another sixty."

Echard knew he couldn't win the argument.

He blamed their losing on the fact that Doc Willis had just driven in from Fort Worth and wasn't up to his normal game. So they all agreed to play again the next morning, and if need be, again the next afternoon.

Doc needed to get in as much work as he could, said John.

Doc and John left the table headed to the men's locker room. John turned and came back.

"By the way, Eloy, can you not call him Green Teeth anymore?" John asked with a defeated look on his face.

"Look at his teeth, Johnny boy. They're green as hell, like he's been chewing on cow turds all day," Eloy said as he stood up from the table. "I think it would improve his appearance if someone knocked all of those green fuckers out of his mouth, don't you?"

John turned immediately to leave as Bonner grabbed the back of Eloy's belt to restrain him.

Everyone met later than evening for a big dinner at the club.

John and Megan were there with Green Teeth. Himey told Eloy there was no way he could ever touch Megan again, just thinking she had screwed old Green Teeth.

"What a revolting thought," Eloy said.

Eloy didn't party as much as he thought he would. When he got home, he poured himself a nightcap and checked his messages on his answering machine.

There was one from Cassie.

He expected it to say, "I'm so miserable without you, it's almost like you're here!" And he was surprised when it didn't.

"Eloy, this is Cassie. I'm sorry I have taken so long to get back to you, but as you probably didn't know, I've been on the road, and when I went to check my answering machine, I found out something was wrong with it. When I dialed in from an outside line, it wouldn't tell me I had messages. I have called you several times, but every time I got your machine. And I really want to talk to you in person, so I didn't leave any messages, but you know, I guess I should have. I really do miss you, and I want us to be together again. I was hoping I would find you tonight to wish you a happy birthday, so happy birthday. But I guess you're at the Member-Guest doing what you love best. You're probably out hitting something hard, like a one iron and a scotch bottle. I sure hope it isn't one of them slinky-kinkies anyway. But listen. One of the music acts for the Amarillo Rodeo had to cancel, and they've asked me to take their place. I am so excited. So I'll be in Amarillo for the rodeo. I do love you, so I'll make you a deal. If you can find me, you can screw me. See you in two weeks."

Oh happy days, thought Eloy.

The next morning was a replay of the previous day—except they did give putts that were in the leather.

John was now looking for anyway he could to get even.

Eloy spoke. "Tell you what I'll do. I'll play you and Green Teeth's low ball this afternoon. My score against your low ball score, one hundred a man."

Doc flinched each time he was called Green Teeth.

Eloy hoped it made him mad. It would be worth getting kicked out of the club to knock every one of those goddamned green teeth out of his head and then stick them up his never wiped ass.

Himey kept talking him out of it. "Just humiliate him in front of everyone," he said. "That'll work better. Fuck him. He ain't worth it. Besides, who would I play with if you had to play Hogan Park all the time?"

Eloy made a mental note to have Triple J blow up Green Teeth's car—with him in it.

John left the table smiling.

Eloy knew before they ever teed off that the afternoon was going to be bad for John and company. John left lunch early to get in some extra practice.

Eloy stood near the bag room, finishing a beer and watching John practice.

It wasn't good.

Eloy just happened to mention he thought John's tempo was a little slower than normal and that it might be the problem with his timing.

John looked like Zorro on the practice tee. You know you're hitting it bad when you throw a club when practicing.

John didn't come back from the afternoon round smiling, plus he was still too stupid to realize that Doc Willis wasn't as good as he bragged about. John was dumb like that.

But what did Doc care? John was paying all of the bets.

They adjusted the afternoon bets.

Himey didn't get any more strokes.

Eloy played their low ball, and both Bonner and Eloy had to give Doc three strokes a side.

As it turned out they probably could have given him six strokes a side and still have won money.

There was a tense moment or two that started on the tenth fairway. Eloy kept seeing Doc bend over in the rough. Eloy thought he was improving the lie of his ball. Finally, on the fifteenth hole, Eloy said, "Johnny boy, remember the R.T. match?"

John looked at Eloy like *What the hell are you talking about?*

A couple of years back, John and R.T. had played a match and Eloy had caught John cheating.

"Better tell fucking Green Teeth over there that the next time he bends over in the rough, he'd better have his goddamned hands in his pockets."

It was another $800 loss for John and Doc.

Bonner said, "Hell, John, you two could go play Pebble Beach for those kinds of rates!"

Eloy and Dad Wilkinson arrived at the Green Tree Country Club Thursday morning at the same time.

Dad was going to get in an early practice round before going to some fancy dinner affair arranged by his wife Sylvia. A "foo-foo affair," Dad called them. He said he'd rather go to the dentist or sit around some new construction and watch paint dry, or cement cure.

They pulled into the Green Tree Country Club parking lot at precisely the same time, Dad from the west entrance and Eloy from the east entrance. They met in the parking lot.

Dad knew Eloy had Echard and Doc scheduled for another day of golf.

As they walked, they briefly talked about how well their oil wells were doing and how fortunate they were for having them.

The club building at Green Tree sat about ten feet above the rest of the terrain. It was built so that the golf cart storage facility was in the lower level of the building. The clubhouse was on the second story and sat about a half a story above the parking lot and the rest of the golf course.

You could get to the pro shop from the main parking lot in front of the building by walking across the parking lot, up a set of stairs, across the covered, circular drive, through the main entry doors, then through the Men's Grill and on to the pro shop. Or you could walk to the right side of the building to a door that led to the men's locker room, through the locker room, and then on to the pro shop. Or you could walk to the right of the building using the cart path that led to the parking lot. Then you could walk up the cart ramp that led to the bag room and on into the pro shop.

Eloy and Dad chose the latter route. They walked up the ramp toward the bag room and the pro shop.

Every time Eloy would see that bench in the bag room, where he had introduced Megan Echard to some limited fancy fucking, he would grin and think that maybe someone should put up a plaque. He could swear that sometimes he could still see the imprint of her ass on the countertop.

They walked up the ramp in time to witness the omen for the day.

John Echard was on the driving range, attempting to hit balls, but basically throwing clubs; whirlybirds were in the air.

Dad turned to Eloy. "Don't you just love the sound of three irons flying through the air early in morning?"

"Looks like his timing is still a little off, don't it?"

Dad punched Eloy in the ribs with his elbow and commented on how it appeared Eloy was going to get his dues paid for the next three months or so.

Eloy responded that he was going for much more than the next three months.

A funny thing happened that afternoon. Doc Green Teeth Willis, the greatest left-handed golfer in the great state of Texas, allowed the choke bug to get in his throat, then—as Eloy would say—he swallowed him whole.

Willie Hickey must have coughed him up.

Himey said the Fina Truck pulled up and loaded Green Teeth with the gas.

Green Teeth hit his tee ball out of bounds on the tenth hole. He then proceeded to tell John how to hit every shot on the tenth hole.

The same thing happened on the eleventh hole. Green Teeth hit his tee ball out of bounds and then he became John's coach.

Now John had two bad swing thoughts in his head on each shot—his and Doc's.

Eloy and Bonner sat back and watched the self-destruction take place.

Ditto on the twelfth hole—OB hit three for Doc.

And when Doc said, "I can't believe you made double bogey on that hole," you could see Echard's face turning red from anger, but he didn't say anything.

Then what occurred on the thirteenth hole both amazed Eloy and Bonner and made them laugh.

Echard aligned his body to the left, aiming at the houses, and hit his tee ball purposely out of bounds. He swung hard and the ball landed on top of one of the rooftops, took a large bounce, landed in the street and bounced across a flowerbed or two, then rattled against one of the houses that lined the fourteenth hole.

Echard turned to Doc and said, "Now, Mr. Fucking Golf Coach, let's see if you can play a hole or two."

After the round was finished, Echard and Doc had lost a combined $3,000. Echard wanted to settle after the jamboree was over.

Eloy wanted Doc's money right then.

Both Echard and Doc wanted to chance to get their money back during the weekend.

Usually, Eloy didn't like team or side bets during a tournament. It was something he usually didn't do. He wanted to concentrate on the tournament and Calcutta, not just one team.

It was Bonner who convinced him they could make more money off Echard and Doc than they could in the Calcutta.

Eloy told Moses he might want to send a spotter out with Doc and John. Moses asked why. They were playing with another team.

"Not good enough," said Eloy. "Green Teeth is slipperier than a used condom!"

Bonner was right about the money. When the tournament was over, John Echard had lost a total of $10,000–$5,000 of it was Doc's money.

Even money by the bookies had it John would never be repaid by Green Teeth.

Sometimes, it was hell when you tried to double up to catch up. Especially when you were not good at betting—and even worse at whatever you were gambling on.

The other good thing for Eloy, as a result of John and Green Teeth losing, was he would never, ever have to see fucking Green Teeth, Doc Percy Willis, again.

Another thing, that weekend ended up being extra bad for Echard. Sunday evening, after the Jamboree, he cornered Dad Wilkinson in the men's locker room.

Echard and Dad were in a business deal together that had gone bad. Given the fact Echard had lost the ten grand gambling, he now wanted Dad to repay him for his lost investment. The sum of the investment just happened to be what he lost to Eloy and company.

They got into a shouting match. John was drunk, and John's first mistake was when he shoved Dad to the floor. Thirty-year old men just shouldn't shove sixty-five-year-old men to the floor. His second mistake was his timing was still too slow—too slow to duck.

Ellis Budde came around the corner and saw John shove Dad to the floor. Ellis, the mean son of a bitch that he was, didn't care who was right or who was wrong, Dad was his friend and John Echard wasn't. Ellis hit John with a perfect right cross. John ended up spending two days in the hospital with a broken jaw and crushed cheekbone.

Eloy told Ellis that he had just cost him two or three months' worth of country club dues. Ellis told Eloy to send him an invoice and he would make sure he got paid. He said it was damn well worth it.

During the practice rounds and the gambling with Green Teeth and Echard, Eloy noticed that Bonner was really good out of the tall Bermuda rough, especially when he used his Spaulding Trouble Lover sand wedge.

Eloy thought that Bonner was better around the greens than R.T., which was saying something.

R.T. held the club too lightly, which was normally good, but not when you're trying to gouge it out of six-inch tall Bermuda grass.

Bonner held the club much more firmly attributing to his excellence out of the rough. If Bonner continued to play this good, and if Eloy could help him, they had a chance at winning the Jamboree.

On Friday, they were paired with R.T. and the Hogan Park MGA champion. His name was Spencer Wampler.

Eloy didn't like that too much because he didn't want to get caught up in beating them and lose sight of the overall scope of the tournament. Somehow, he and Bonner managed to stay focused and shoot a sixty-five. R.T. and Spencer shot a sixty-seven. They were in first and third place after day one.

They all met that night at Eloy's for dinner and drinks. With Cassie missing, it just didn't seem like old times.

Kathy Wahl had stayed at the pool all afternoon to work on her perfect tan on the outside and a perfect drunk on the inside. She was just tittering drunk. She almost couldn't walk, yet she could. It didn't make any difference to R.T., as long as she left him alone so he could concentrate on his golf. And R.T. really liked Kathy because, unlike Cheryl Gail, Kathy had her own money. Though sometimes, when she wanted him to buy her something expensive and he refused, she still called him a cheap, tight-assed son of a bitch.

Kathy came to Eloy's house dressed in tight blue jeans and a fresh-starched, yellow, sleeveless blouse. She had on black cowboy boots that came almost up to her knees, and her jeans were tucked inside her boots. She had on a black leather belt studded with diamonds. She looked good and smelled even better.

Eloy knew what R.T. liked in her. She had this certain classiness about her.

Kathy Wahl, in the state she was in, was unencumbered and uninhibited. Someone just happened to mentioned Spook's name. To anyone who would listen, she said, "You girls are too enamored with the size of a man's dick. You all know that you can get more done with one inch of tongue than you can with ten inches of dick! Using that tongue for something other than making a smart-assed remark could add something to your repertoire for fancy fucking, right, Eloy boy?"

Eloy looked at Kathy with a sly smile.

The rest of them looked stunned.

She saw the look on their faces and knew she had made a small mistake. She got this sheepish grin on her face. "Anyway, it does for me."

Saturday's round was another good one for Bonner and Eloy. It was an even better one for R.T. and Spencer. Bonner and Eloy shot another sixty-five, but R.T. and Spencer tied them for the lead with a sixty-three. They would be paired together for Sunday's final round.

Eloy was nervous and excited. He had never won the Green Tree Country Club Jamboree. He felt really good about his and Bonner's chances.

They all met at the club Saturday night for the Jamboree cocktails, dinner, and dance.

Himey and Eloy ran into Himey's ex-wife, Barbara, at the bar when they were getting drinks.

"Did you feel it?" asked Himey.

"Feel what?"

"When she walked up, the temperature dropped about ten degrees." Then Himey broke into song with the tune of "How the Grinch Stole Christmas." "She's a cold one, Mrs. Bitch."

"You guys finally get everything settled on the divorce?" asked Eloy.

"As the days go by, I think of how lucky I am that she's not here to ruin it for me. Every time someone says, 'Let's go get a cold one,' I think of old Barb first, Miller Lite second. You know how to kill a good hard-on, don't you, Eloy?"

Eloy waited for the answer.

"Just get a good look at old Barb naked."

Eloy laughed.

"You know the difference between a wife and a girlfriend, E?"

"Forty-five pounds?"

"There you go."

Eloy attended the Calcutta. It was held in the garage of a private residence. Green Tree Country Club didn't support or approve of Calcutta's, so they were not allowed on the premises. He stayed long enough for the Championship Flight to be sold. He bought himself and Bonner and also R.T. and Spencer. How could he go wrong?

After he paid for the two teams he purchased, the tiredness hit Eloy. He went home. He had a good, stiff nightcap and was in bed by 9:30 p.m. He hoped no one saw him leave early—he didn't want to ruin his reputation. He drifted off into dreams.

In his dream, Eloy could see the outline of the courses from his window seat in the first-class section of the American Airlines airplane. He had been here before and had played all of the courses on the Monterey Peninsula, but not under these circumstances.

When the plane landed and he gathered his bags, he had a limousine take him to his hotel.

When the white limousine pulled into Seventeen Mile Drive, Eloy started to get excited.

Here he was—an amateur—at the US Open. And he wasn't a spectator either; he had qualified through the Regional Qualifying Tournament in Texas and earned his rightful place as a full-fledged contestant.

He was due for a practice round on Monday with Tom Kite and John Adams.

As the limo neared the Pebble Beach Lodge, he saw the Pacific Ocean crashing its waves against the cliffs of the eighteenth hole of the Pebble Beach Golf Links. It brought a knot to his stomach. How in the hell was he going to do this without throwing up? He had the urge to tell the driver to turn the limo around and get him the hell out of here before he hurt someone or embarrassed himself to death.

He couldn't even imagine the pressure of coming to that majestic eighteenth hole with a chance to win the US Open. How the hell do the pros even draw it back and make a good swing in that situation?

His practice rounds with Tom Kite, John Adams, and others settled his nerves some, but as they said in Texas, he was still as jumpy as a road lizard on a hot road in heavy traffic.

None of his rounds produced anything great, but he did learn some good course management from Kite and from one round with Jack Nicklaus. The round with Nicklaus alone was worth the $6,000 or $7,000 this was costing him.

During the Wednesday practice round with Tom Kite, Tom looked at Eloy's wedges and quickly informed Eloy that they weren't suited for the type of turf and sand at Pebble Beach.

Tom got Eloy a pitching wedge and sand wedge from the Wilson Staff PGA Tour representative. It was a kind gesture, one Eloy would never forget.

The first round on Thursday was incredible. Nerves and all, Eloy shot a sixty-five, He laughed when he yip-hit a short putt and it went in the hole. One hell of a good score anywhere, but this was the US Open at Pebble Beach. It might have been the best round of golf Eloy ever played.

He holed his second shot on the par-four fourth hole for an eagle two—just like he had done in Friona. God bless the new pitching wedge Tom Kite had gotten for him.

As normal, the headlines read, UNKNOWN LEADS US OPEN. The headline was true. Eloy wouldn't have cared if the headline read, SHITHEAD LEADS US OPEN or YIP-HITTING DRUNK LEADS THE US OPEN.

In the pressroom after the round, he tried to be charming and witty, but he was scared to death and it was hard to think and talk when you had shit in your neck—and Mr. Dewar's was AWOL. He was choking worse here than on the golf course. He was certain the press had passed him off as just another lucky redneck Texan.

He knew Dan Jenkins did. Jenkins only liked Hogan or Nicklaus or Trevino. He thought all the others else were just hackers getting in the way. If Dan Jenkins had his way, each tournament would only have three or four entrants.

Eloy was right. He was a lucky redneck Texan, and if they didn't like it, then fuck 'em. Let them work for a living and see how good they could play.

The second round Friday at the US Open wasn't as good as Thursday's. How could it be? But then Eloy might not ever again play as good as he had on Thursday. But he did manage to turn in a seventy-two and was tied for the lead with Dr. Gil Morgan.

In the pressroom, Eloy mentioned that it might be the battle of the Red River again, being that Dr. Gil Morgan was from Oklahoma and Eloy was from Texas. The press didn't seem to think that was too humorous since there were still two rounds to go. They thought it rather brash that Eloy would even bring it to their attention. And Eloy was an unknown amateur, and Dr. Gil Morgan was a bona fide touring professional with multiple wins on the PGA Tour. He could normally give Eloy three shots for nine holes and dust his ass.

It must be true, Eloy thought, *because that's what Jenkins wrote the next day in the paper.*

Dr. Gill plus a whole world of other players better than Eloy were only a few strokes behind. Guys like Tom Watson, Jack Nicklaus, and Tom Kite were always lurking somewhere in the neighborhood when a major golf tournament was being conducted.

And another thing . . . Every time Eloy played with Tom Kite back at Green Tree in Midland, Tom always won, so how was Eloy going to beat him now?

Hell, even Judy Rankin beat Eloy at Green Tree. Of course, she beat all the men there, every one of them.

Saturday started off bad for Eloy. He made a double bogey on the first hole. Then to suffer more injury, he made a double bogey on the easiest hole on the course, the par-five second hole.

He was four over par and headed south.

But he didn't throw clubs, he didn't get mad, and he didn't cuss where any of the blue-coated officials could hear him. He did that in a Porta-Potty next to the third tee. He also threw up. And to make things worse, a piece of bell pepper from his morning omelet got stuck in his nose. He had to smell that damn bell pepper for two or three holes before he finally blew it out. It must have helped somehow though, because he finished the round with two birdies and turned in a respectable seventy-four.

The headlines no longer read, UNKNOWN LEADS THE US OPEN. Eloy was now in second place. Tom Watson was in the lead.

It was hard for Eloy to sleep that night. He flipped and flopped. Each time he rolled over, he would look at the clock, hoping it was time to get up. Each time he looked, he had only slept one hour.

Sunday morning came and Eloy felt at peace with himself. He looked out of his hotel window and saw the wind was blowing like hell. It was misting rain, and the fog was thick; some called it a pea-soup fog.

Perfect, he thought. Most of the field would be eliminated with these conditions, but not him. Hell, back at home, they played in the wind and bad weather all of the time. Maybe that was why he had played badly on Saturday—the wind wasn't blowing.

Eloy was paired with Tom Watson for the final round. He was extremely nervous and was shaking like a dog shitting a peach seed on the first tee. How he hit that first tee ball, he'd never know. He just stood there, frozen, staring blankly at the fairway.

The marshal had to nudge him to get him to move.

Eloy and Tom matched score for score for the first seven holes. Then Eloy got into a tie for the lead when somehow, miraculously, he chipped in for a birdie from the right side of the eighth green.

Most people made double bogey from the right side of number eight at Pebble Beach.

He was below the level of the green, on the steep side of the hill leading to the Pacific Ocean, and couldn't even see the pin, so he hit the best shot he could and was damn lucky—he had just turned a six into a three. Tom Kite's sand wedge gift hit the miraculous shot.

Eloy kissed the sand wedge as he took the ball out of the hole.

He looked at Watson. Watson just slightly grinned and tipped his hat.

He looked at the scoreboard as he left the eighth green and saw that Nicklaus was now only one shot behind. *Goddamn*, he thought, *how the hell can I beat both of them?* And he said so to his caddie.

He was reminded by his caddie on the ninth tee that he wasn't playing their best ball and if he wanted to lose—just keep thinking about it.

When they arrived at the seventeenth hole, Eloy had a one stroke margin over Watson and a two-stroke margin over Nicklaus.

Eloy had the honors on the seventeenth tee. He had 194 yards to the pin with the stiff Pacific wind blowing into his face. He chose his one iron, settled into his stance, but then abruptly backed off.

His caddie approached with the bag.

Eloy waved him off. Eloy was visualizing the shot Nicklaus had hit on the seventeenth hole when he won the US Open a few years back.

He settled in again, made one of his best swings of the day, and hit his ball on a boring trajectory toward the pin.

The ball was hit so solidly the wind didn't affect its flight. It stopped ten feet from the hole.

The gallery around the tee gave him a huge cheer.

Watson hit his tee ball into the left rough, pin high, beside the green.

Eloy figured Watson was dead.

Watson studied his lie very carefully.

Eloy's caddie said, "He be dead. He be lookin' up the bogey man's ass."

At the same time, Eloy overheard Tom tell his caddie he was going to chip it in the hole for a birdie. *Fat chance,* thought Eloy.

Then Watson took his sand wedge, made this beautiful little swing, and popped the ball out of the tall grass.

They all watched it as it hit the green, grabbed the grass with its teeth, then rolled slowly toward the hole and disappeared into the bottom of the cup for a birdie. Watson ran around the green pumping his arms.

Eloy never moved, he never wavered, but under his breath, he said, "Lucky little sum-bitch."

Eloy's caddie said, "Sum-bitch, boss. Got to answer him now."

Eloy wondered if Kite had given Watson a Wilson Staff sand wedge too.

After Watson and the crowd settled down, Eloy set the Tommy Armour IM5 putter behind the ball, steeled his nerves, and calmly stroked the ten-foot putt into the hole for a birdie of his own. He still had his one-shot lead!

The crowd didn't go as wild about his birdie as they had about Watson's. Eloy mentioned this to his caddie. He said it was just like back home. His caddie told him on the eighteenth tee that he wasn't here to get claps, just birdies. He said the crowd was prejudiced, just didn't take kindly to unknown rednecks that talked funny. He also said the crowd could just go fuck themselves. Best he could recall, a crowd never won nothing.

Eloy agreed. "Fuck 'em if they can't take a birdie."

Eloy stood on the eighteenth tee and remembered his feelings the day he drove in. He now understood it wasn't as hard as he thought it would be when you were in the heat of the battle. He made his backswing, took the club to the top, braced his left arm, and made a perfect swing.

Eloy and Watson both hit perfect drives. They each hit excellent approach shots. They hit wedge shots to the green. They both had makeable birdie putts.

Watson was a few feet farther away from the hole than Eloy. Watson putted first; it was a true roll. He calmly made his putt and birdied the eighteenth hole.

Now Eloy had to make another tricky putt to win—and calmness was nowhere to be found for Eloy. As Eloy surveyed his putt, his first thought was that he hoped his hand wouldn't flinch and knock his ball somewhere out into the Pacific Ocean. He didn't need another yip-hit right now. But someone was smiling on Eloy's hands that day. They didn't shake, and they didn't flinch. Eloy could see them as if they were in slow motion. His hands remained steady, and they made the perfect stroke.

It seemed as if the ball took several minutes to reach the hole. It paused, and then fell in. *Bam!* Eloy was now the US Open champion.

Nicklaus, playing behind them, didn't have a chance.

Fucking A, he thought! And he said so to his caddie, who was dancing a jig on the fringe with one of the marshals.

Everyone was in shock, especially Eloy. The crowd was in shock, so much that at first they didn't clap. Then slowly, ever so slowly, one by one, they broke into applause. It was Tom Kite who had clapped first, then Nicklaus from the fairway, then Watson. Then the crowd started clapping, and they started to chant, "The Breeze, The Breeze."

Eloy just stood there stunned and didn't move, until Tom Watson came over to congratulate him.

As he walked off the green, Tom Kite shook his hand and said, "Nice wedges, huh?"

Jack Nicklaus found Eloy after he finished his round and offered his congratulations.

In the pressroom, everyone was patting him on the back and giving him accolades. But each time someone in the press corps would ask him a question, he was interrupted by a phone ringing. Here he was in the grandest moment of his life, and this damn phone was destroying his limelight. Goddamn it. Couldn't the USGA find a flunky to answer a damn phone, especially at a moment like this? Where in the hell was Himey when you needed him.

Dan Jenkins was asking him a question, and when he was about to reply, there went the damn phone again. Ringing, ringing, and ringing.

"Excuse me," said Eloy. "Let me get rid of this damn ringing in my ear."

Eloy reached and fumbled for the phone. The phone found his hand. That's when he awoke. He sat up in bed dazed, stunned. Then he realized he was reaching for the phone on the nightstand beside his bed.—not in Pebble Beach.

He was disoriented at first. *What the hell is going on here?* Then he realized he was at his house and not in Pebble Beach.

It was Dad calling, wanting to go to breakfast.

He got out of bed, went to the window, and peered through the curtain to check the weather, clearing his head. *Now that was one hell of a dream,* he thought—the best dream he'd ever had. That was even better than dreaming about Jo Beth Tucker back in high school, dreaming she was naked hanging from a rafter giving him a blowjob. Even better than *all* of the women of the world he had dream-fucked.

He made some coffee and sat down on the sofa. Too bad, he thought. Too bad he didn't really have the talent to make it come true, but nonetheless, it made him feel good about himself. He wondered if going to bed half-sober would produce a dream like that each night. If so, he might have to consider giving up drinking.

Looking out the window, he saw the wind was blowing and that it was overcast and misting, just like in the dream. He knew if he could beat Watson and Nicklaus in conditions like that, then hell, today would be a cakewalk; he could beat all the players that were playing in the Jamboree.

That's what he thought, and using that frame of mind, that's exactly what he did.

Eloy felt the best he had in months on that Sunday morning. The dream had him in the best of moods, and he was well rested. As he hit balls on the range warming up for the final round, it was so simple, just like Billy Clyde said it would be.

His swing fell into the *groove*, and just like in the dream, it felt good, real good. He had the feeling that his right shoulder went down and through the ball. The ball's flight, the trajectory, was perfect. He hit seven iron after seven iron, and they all had the same feeling. They rose into the gray mist and at their apex moved about one yard left.

He took out his driver, hit the first ball, and it felt the same. His swing felt real good.

He looked in his bag and there were the two Wilson Staff wedges he had gotten from Tom Kite a couple of years back. He knew now that they must have some magic in them.

R.T., Spencer, Bonner, and Eloy were the last group to play in Sunday's final round of the Jamboree.

Moses Jenks introduced them over the loud speaker. "Ladies and gentlemen, for the last tee time of the 1985 Green Tree County Club Jamboree, the first team to play is Mr. R.T. Deacon, former Texas State Amateur champion, and the Hogan Park Men's Golf Association champion, Mr. Spencer Wampler."

The few who were on the putting green or around the first tee politely gave applause.

R.T. and Spencer hit their tee shots.

"Next to play is Mr. Bonner Bennet, a perennial champion and member of the Bar-B-Que Circuit Hall of Fame, and the notorious, not famous, E.B. Breeze."

Sunday's round produced some good golf by both teams.

After the first nine holes, they were still tied thanks to a remarkable shot and putt by Eloy.

The ninth hole was a par-five, and if you were to hit the green in two shots, the second shot must carry a small pond in front of the green.

Eloy hit his tee shot where he normally did.

Bonner decided to lay up short of the small pond.

Eloy never hesitated. He took his three-wood and made the best swing he could. The ball flew high and straight and stayed straight, but it needed to move some to the left to fully clear the small pond.

"You need to move some for me, ball. Come on now," said Eloy quietly. He was hoping it would clear the small pond. "Ain't no time to be hittin' a straight ball, boy," he said aloud.

The ball hit next to the yellow water hazard stake marking the boundary of the small pond, then miraculously bounced forward and ran onto the green.

Eloy made the twenty-foot putt for an eagle three.

It was now apparent that it would be one of these two teams that would win the Jamboree.

It was to be either Bonner and Eloy or R.T. and Spencer.

The lead changed hands several times, depending on who made the last birdie.

Spencer chipped in for a birdie on the seventeenth hole to give him and R.T. a one-shot lead going to the last hole.

He looked at Eloy, grinned, and said, "New wedge. More bounce. Replaced it after that debacle at Hogan."

Damn, thought Eloy, *am I to be runner-up again?*

Each player hit their drive in the middle of the fairway on the par-five finishing hole. R.T. was the first to play his second shot and missed the green, short and to the right. Spencer hit his second shot into the bunker greenside bunker.

Bonner managed to get his second shot barely onto the front of the green.

The pin on the eighteenth hole that Sunday was located in the back left portion of the green.

Eloy hit a nice high four iron that drew slightly and settled some twenty-five feet below the hole.

R.T. chipped to within three feet.

Spencer's bunker shot stopped about five feet from the hole.

Eloy and Bonner knew that either R.T. or Spencer would make their putt for a birdie. One of them had to make the putt for an eagle or go home runner-up again.

Eloy remembered a few years ago when he had three-putted and R.T. had missed a three-footer and they had lost the tournament. He certainly didn't think R.T. would miss this three-foot putt. No way would he miss again.

Bonner hit his forty-foot putt toward the hole.

Ely thought it was going to go in. *Come on, get luck, and win this bitch for me,* he thought.

It hit the hole, caught the lip, and spun around 360 degrees before stopping six inches away.

Bonner said as loud as he could, "Well, gawdddd-damn, lipping bitch." And then he walked up and tapped it in for his birdie.

Those few people who were watching flinched.

Eloy had watched Bonner's putt, especially right at the end. He had a perfect read on the line the ball needed to roll. It was now for the hard part of the putt—getting the right speed.

Bonner walked behind Eloy and put his hand on Eloy's shoulder. "It's time to take out the trash, baby."

Eloy concentrated as hard as he could and hit his best putt.

Going up the hill, the ball slowed enough you could read TITLEIST on each revolution.

Eloy held his breath thinking he hit it too easy, but it kept rolling.

"Dig, bitch, dig," Bonner said.

The ball was moving as slowly as Eloy's breath when it rolled into the center of the cup.

Eagle!

Bonner ran over to the hole, retrieved the ball from the bottom of the cup, spread his legs, and then rubbed the ball on his crotch. "There's some big sugar for ya, Eloy," said Bonner.

No one knew where that habit got started, but players in the panhandle and West Texas did it all of the time. If their partner made a big putt, the other one would get the ball out of the hole and then "give it some sugar" by rubbing it back and forth on their crotch. Eloy had never seen a woman golfer perform such an act.

Now the pressure was back on. R.T. and Spencer; one of them had to make their putt to tie. Spencer didn't leave it up to R.T. He calmly stroked his ball into the middle of the hole. It was now time for sudden-death playoff.

The playoff for the championship started on the first hole, a short dogleg-right par-four. The playoff didn't last long. After a nice drive in the middle of the fairway, Eloy hit his wedge shot two feet from the hole for an easy birdie.

R.T. and Spencer could only manage pars, although R.T. hit a putt that should have gone in—but didn't.

Bonner said afterward, "Wonder what kept that out!"

"White, kryptonic voodoo," said Eloy.

Eloy was finally on the winning team. He had finally won the Jamboree.

One other thing that made the Jamboree bad for John Echard, other than losing $10,000 and having his jaw broken, was that he had bet on R.T. to win.

Eloy and Bonner didn't party long for their celebration. Bonner needed to get back to Amarillo as soon as possible. Eloy told him it was okay. He would drink enough for the both of them and if Bonner didn't hear from him in a week or so, he should call the missing persons bureau.

In the clubhouse while having a couple of drinks, R.T. told Eloy, "Congratulations. That was the best I've ever seen you play."

"Thanks," said Eloy.

He handed R.T. an envelope. It contained their winnings from the Calcutta minus what Eloy had paid for the team. It was a most generous gesture by Eloy. Eloy was happy. It would take a week for his smile to disappear.

CHAPTER 8

Eloy drove to the south side of Lubbock. He wanted some chicken gizzards with hot, spicy, barbecue sauce from Pinky's Liquor and Drive-In located on the Lubbock Strip on Highway 87. One couldn't buy alcohol in the city limits of Lubbock. Some kind of Baptist thing some said, so all the Baptists had to drive south of town to the Lubbock Strip to buy their beer and whiskey.

Eloy got a dozen chicken gizzards covered with the hot, spicy, barbeque sauce and an eight-pack of Miller Lite Little Hitlers. Little Hitlers was what Bonner called the Miller Lite eight-ounce bottles of beer.

While he waited to pay at the checkout counter, his thoughts were on how he was going to get all that money from Willie and Weldon. He had collected a little bit, but there was a considerable amount still due and payable, "on the jawbone" as they said sometimes. The jawbone was, "Yes, I owe you, but I'll have to catch you later, beings I'm broke."

The money didn't really matter. What really mattered was that his game was good again, Cassie was coming to Amarillo, and he felt good about himself. Ying and yang, shit, fuck—all in balance.

As he left the building, someone calling his name interrupted his thoughts. He looked up to see Adie Connors walking toward the door.

"Well, if it isn't E.B. Breeze. How have you been?"

"I'm good, Adie. And you?"

"Oh, just supporting the hubby. He's running for office again."

"Damn, I'm surprised I didn't smell you first. Losing your touch?"

"Been running here and there. That perfume is special," said Adie, "You staying over tonight at the Villa?"

"No. On the way to Amarillo, golf and such, meeting my girlfriend. Haven't seen her in a while."

"What are you doing for the next couple of hours?"

"Sorry, got a girlfriend now, involved."

"Involved? Me too, but I'm not looking to get married, hon. Just a frolic between two friends."

Eloy shrugged his shoulders.

"Look for me sometimes at The Bar." With that, Adie Connors turned and walked to her car.

Eloy watched her walk away. What a nice body.

Eloy was proud of himself for not succumbing to the temptations of Adie. Maybe there was hope for him yet.

He wasn't in a hurry to get to Amarillo.

Cassie didn't start singing at the rodeo until nine o'clock that evening, and she wouldn't want to engage in frivolous activities before her show.

And for him, once he got her naked, she wasn't getting dressed again unless it was to go buy him more scotch.

He got his golf towel from the trunk, positioned the chicken gizzards and Little Hitlers on the passenger side front seat, put the Mercedes in gear, and then leisurely eased onto the highway.

He found a Jerry Lee Lewis song, "I'll Get It Where I Can," on the radio and turned it up loud.

He popped a chicken gizzard in his mouth, chewed the perfectly cooked meat, and savored the flavors. He then drank down half of the first Little Hitler.

He listened to Jerry Lee, ate the gizzards, and drank the Little Hitlers. He liked the line in the song that said if I can't get it at home, I'll get it anywhere I can.

Eloy continued to eat the gizzards and drink the Little Hitlers. He used his golf towel for a bib, being careful not to get the hot, spicy, barbeque sauce on his shirt or pants. He was trying to time it just right so the gizzards and the beer ran out at the same time. He wasn't doing a bad job.

Eloy wished he had written the song for Jerry Lee. It sounded like something he might come up with. Just like him, if I can't get it at home, I'll get it anywhere I can. *Perfect*, he thought.

As Eloy got to the edge of Plainview, Texas, another song came on the radio: "Call Me the Breeze," by Lynyrd Skynyrd. This song gave him a feeling of euphoria. What a good theme song to go with his new name, E.B. Breeze. He turned the radio up loud so he could feel the bass and the beat in his chest. He was like Weldon. He was invincible.

He sang the song as loud as he could sing. He changed some of the words to suit himself. "They call me the breeze. I keep blowing' down the road. Well, now they call me the breeze. I'm as free as the wind. I do only as I please. They call me the breeze."

How fitting for me. "Ain't got me no burdens. I'm fast and loose as can be. Ain't got me no burdens. I'm as fast and loose as can be. Ain't hiding from nobody, Cassie ain't hiding from me."

His mind drifted to Cassie. He didn't hear the rest of the lyrics to the song, only the upscale beat. As the song ended, he popped the last gizzard into his mouth, savored the taste, and then took a drink of his last Little Hitler.

A song by ZZ Top, "La Grange," then sprang to life on the radio. It was one of Eloy's favorites. He turned it up loud. He was happy, and his foot pressed hard on the accelerator. The Mercedes responded and rocketed along the highway. He would have pressed the accelerator farther, but the floor of the car got in the way.

He went so fast he didn't remember going through Happy, Texas.

Eloy's heavy foot and the good music got him to Amarillo earlier than expected. He saw the exit sign that pointed to the Southwest Golf Club and decided in an instant to see if Bonner Bennet was there.

He took the exit at full speed, slammed on the brakes, banked hard left, and skid around the corner.

Then he rammed the gas pedal to the floor and quickly drove the mile or so to the Southwest Golf Club. He found a parking spot near the front door.

He headed straight for the men's room before going into the pro shop. Peeing after holding it so long always felt good. He finished and made his way to the pro shop.

"Have you seen Bonner Bennet?" Eloy asked the person behind the sales counter.

"Just left a few minutes ago."

"Any idea where he went?" Eloy asked.

"I think he hangs out at Stumpy's nowadays."

"Stumpy's? Where's that?"

"Sixteenth and Washington."

"Isn't that where the Sixteenth Avenue Lounge is?"

"Yep, across the parking lot."

Eloy traveled north on the Canyon freeway into Amarillo to the Washington Street exit. Then he headed across Interstate 40 to Sixteenth Avenue and turned right.

Hell, thought Eloy, *this is the same way you go to get to the Sixteenth Avenue Lounge.*

He pulled into the same parking lot where the Sixteenth Avenue Lounge was located.

Eloy looked to his right and saw Stumpy's.

He looked to his left and there was the Sixteenth Avenue Lounge.

The two bars couldn't have been more than seventy-five yards apart. The Sixteenth Avenue Lounge sat on the east side of the potholed, dirt parking lot. Stumpy's sat on the west side.

Eloy pulled the Mercedes into the safest spot he could find, got out of his car, and went inside Stumpy's to find Bonner.

He walked through the back door and waited a moment for his eyes to adjust to the darkness of the room. Then he saw Bonner and Spook Thompson sitting at the bar.

Before they greeted each other, Eloy asked, "Why did you change bars? What's the difference? They're both right here together," he said to the both of them.

"It's better in here," answered Bonner.

"How's that?"

"Hell, Eloy. The Sixteenth is in a bad neighborhood," said Spook.

They were interrupted by someone clanging a spoon or fork on a beer bottle.

Another man seated at the bar asked, "Anyone in here know the difference between John Wayne and Jack Daniels?"

Eloy thought hard but he didn't know the difference. He didn't even know what they had in common.

There was a long silence as they all waited for someone to give the answer.

Finally, the man said, "Jack Daniels is still killing Indians."

Eloy arrived at the Amarillo Fair Grounds Rodeo arena just about 9:30 p.m.

He bought his ticket at the front gate and then worked his way through the crowd to the end of the rodeo arena where Cassie would be exiting. He was going to make sure he she made good on her promise. She had said that if he found her then he could screw her. Well, hide-and-seek was over, and she'd better be ready for a first-class, A#1 Pompeii, because one or two was coming her way.

She came onstage. She was gorgeous! Someone beside Eloy remarked, "Now that's a woman!" She looked good onstage, and she sounded even better, better than Eloy remembered.

Eloy was proud. She sang his song, "Just Getting Romantic by Myself" for her closing number.

Eloy walked up to Cassie as she was coming down the stairs from the portable stage. He grabbed her, and before she could say anything, he gave her a long and passionate kiss.

When their lips separated, she said, "Well, if it isn't Eloy, not famous but notorious, Baines. You know, I must have forgotten I was trying to forget about you."

"That train runs on both sides of the tracks now, doesn't it?"

Cassie grinned and nodded her head yes. "I'm just glad it was you, 'cause it made me horny. How goes things on the barbeque circuit?"

"It's just West Texas livin' and T-shirt-wearing women."

"Sounds like a song title to me. But it should be 'Big-Chested Women.'"

"Maybe, but not all women in West Texas are well endowed as some we know. Hell, flat-chested girls need to get a little too."

"Hasn't changed, huh? Golf, hard booze, and soft women?"

"Nope, we still go at it long and we go at it strong. And you know we all still play from the back tees."

"Yep, and I bet you still drink from them too!"

Eloy grinned and said, "Damned if we don't! Got any in your pocket?"

Cassie looked at him and grinned. "You ever think about quitting?"

Eloy laughed and replied, "Now Cassie, you know no one likes a quitter."

"I believe that saying is for sports, not drinking or smoking or chasing faithless women!"

"Oh, you mean quit golf? Hell, I can't quit golf. I wouldn't have a reason to drink then."

"You know I'm glad I don't like golf, because if I did, I would do it, and then I would hate it," remarked Cassie.

"Just like me," said Eloy. "But now that I have found you, where do you want me to have you?"

Cassie gave Eloy another long, gentle kiss. When she released him, she said, "Civilized or uncivilized?"

Eloy knew exactly what she meant. It was an uncivilized sex comment that had gotten him in trouble once back in Tennessee. He made the comment that humans were the only species of animal that had sex behind closed doors. That led to a vigorous discussion among the artichoke crowd that ended with, "He's a fucking caveman. Forget it. Can't argue with argue with a Neanderthal."

"Hell, kid, you pick it. I'm in."

"You would, wouldn't you? Just have me jump up on the hood of that Chevy pickup over there and have me in front of God and everybody? You wouldn't care, would you? What do you think normal people would think?"

"Well, in your case, it would ruin your reputation. For me, it would only enhance mine."

"I guess you have some sound reasoning for that, don't you?"

"Yep, it's like this. Something like that would probably put me in the legendary-class status and right into the hall of fame on the barbeque circuit. All those circuit players, they like shit like that. And then when we're old they would point to me and say, 'There goes old Eloy. He got some on the hood of a Chevy one time at the Amarillo rodeo, with the best-looking female singer you have ever seen. Damn, man, I wish I could do that—lucky fucker.' But when they saw you, they would just point to you and say, 'There goes the Rodeo slut!'"

"Well, hell Eloy, why wouldn't any nice girl want that? But sorry, we have a problem. I have a visitor."

Eloy looked around in all directions. He didn't see anyone special. "Fuck 'em. Show 'em to me and I'll get rid of 'em."

"No, not that kind. My monthly visitor."

Eloy got this hurt look on his face. "Well, shit. Fuck me to tears. I never have been able to whip PMS's ass."

"No, but you've waited this long, another couple of days won't hurt. You have been waiting, haven't you? Or is that a dumb question?"

"Just been getting romantic with myself these days," said Eloy, avoiding the question.

"You know, there was a song written about that. I know the author."

"Yeah, me too."

"Really?"

"Yep, I can shit in his pants!"

Cassie laughed.

"Hell, and I was hoping for some TUFF," said Eloy.

"TUFF? Is that some new acronym for some deviant sexual behavior?"

"Yeah, tear-up-the-furniture fuck!"

"It figures. Only you would come up with something like that." Eloy laughed.

"Eloy, everyone else has to work for a living or is busy worrying about working for a living. All you have to do is drive around and play golf and make up stuff like that."

Eloy laughed. "Well, it is good work if you can get it. But there aren't that many positions available. Only two I know of, and me and Bonner got 'em both."

Then he changed the subject. "You're looking good and happy, so I guess you're handling the PMS thing okay, huh?"

Cassie responded, "Better. But be careful now. You know how I am. Normally, I'm attracted to you. But during PMS, I am more prone to want to shove some scissors through your temple and a one iron up your ass. But you're in luck this time. It's almost over. But I see you're still into the fuck and shit thing."

"Shit and fuck, ying and yang. The guys and I were just discussing that a while back. You know, there are proper times one can say *fuck*."

"Really?"

"No shit. Like, are you going to fuck me or what?"

Cassie grinned. She knew she had said that to Eloy. At the time, it did seem the proper thing to say.

"Or like what JFK said," Eloy continued. "I need another parade like I need a fucking hole in my head."

Cassie rolled her eyes in disgust.

Eloy couldn't help himself. He got this mischievous grin on his face, looked Cassie in the eyes, gave her a little kiss, and said, "Do you have lockjaw too?"

Over coffee at Cassie's house that Tuesday morning, Eloy wrote out a song. He showed it to Cassie.

A Song about Life

It's a song about life.
It's a song about me.
It's about West Texas livin',
T-shirt-wearin' women,
Runnin' in the fast lane, and being a little insane.
It's about backseat sport lovin',
Passions hot as an oven,
Hittin' the wall from alcohol and playing those little
    games.
It's a song about life,
It's a song about me.
I got the windows rolled down, the wind in my hair.
Sipping on a cold one, sitting by a hot one,
With nowhere to go and all day to get there.
It's about West Texas livin',
T-shirt wearin' women,
Being in the fast lane, and being a little insane.
It's a song about life,
It's a song about me.
My wife ran off with a woman, so where did I go
    wrong?
Sipping on a cold one, sitting by a hot one.
She'll be the next, 'cause it won't last too long.
It's about West Texas livin', hot lovin' women,
Working hard on a job, just tryin' to make
    ends meet.
It's about neighborhood sport lovin'
Passions hot as an oven, and trying to get a girl Texas
    sweet.
It's a song about life,
It's a song about me.

"I still think it ought to be Big-Chested women."
Eloy didn't respond. He kissed her on the forehead.

Then he finished his coffee and left the house to meet Bonner.

Eloy got out of the Mercedes Tuesday at noon at the Ross Rogers Golf Course. The first person he saw was Triple J—Jesse Jack Jr.—a hustler, an opportunist, and a golfer. Some said he was a dope dealer. Eloy, like most, called him Triple J for short.

"Say, Trip, what it is?" said Eloy.

Triple J shuffled, hip-hop walked over to Eloy, and shook his hand. "It ain't nothin' wich you, less you done brung Mr. Ups wich ya."

"Mr. Ups?"

"Uh-huh! Don't be pickin' on me without 'em." Triple J went to Eloy's Mercedes and looked in the window. "You got the boy hidin' out in the car there somewhere?"

"Naw, I left Mr. Three Up in Lubbock with Willie Hickey. Mr. Two Up got out in Plainview, and Mr. One Up got off at Hunsley Hills in Canyon, had a game there he said. So I guess Mr. Even Up is the only one showing up today."

"Then you won't be seeing none of my black-assed action, E man. Even wid my partner, Sunshine Ray, I ain't fuckin' wich ya without Mr. Ups on my side. I be slidin' on to sumthin' else, huh, something easy. I done heard what you wrought on to my boy Willie. Laid some serious mojo on his ass. Wudn't nat-u-rell what run across't him—all them eagles and shit. I heard you took all his money—even his mama's rent money. You know that ain't right, just cruel shit, E. A white man takin' a poor black boy's mama's rent money. Cold hearted. Looks like you done got a new ride with the Georges."

"Huh, didn't win that much. Hell, Trip what I won from Willie won't even pay the insurance on that car. Besides, you can't take all a man's money, less he gives it to you. All of Willie's money is still on the jawbone. We kinda roughed up *Well-don* and the dancing man too, but at least the dancing man paid. *Well-don* is still a bit light."

"It's okay to rough up the *Well-don*. He's a h'ain't.

"You mean a ghost?"

"Nope. I mean he h'ain't really black, h'ain't really white, h'ain't really a man. He don't make no marks when he's got cleats on. You see what I mean?"

"You saying he's a little light in the loafers?"

"That's it, that's it. Shiiiiit, E. That boy likes the booty better than the duty, huh? You catch that? *Well-don* be light, get my drift? Like the little semi white honky muthafucker damn near be float-tin."

Eloy saw Bonner outside of the pro shop, cleaning the grips of his golf clubs. Eloy joined him. "I saw Triple J in the parking lot. He's avoiding me like a uniformed cop. Says they're not playing us today."

"Aw hell. I'll get a game with 'em. I'll make it look like he's got the edge. Triple J's got to have the edge."

"Who's Sunshine Ray? Triple J says he is his new partner."

"I've played him a couple of times. No problem, pal."

"Why do they call him Sunshine Ray"?

"'Cause he be smiling all the time."

"Why don't they just call him Smiley or something like that?"

"He's got this gold tooth right in front. And it looks like the sun is always shining right out of his mouth."

You know, it scared Eloy to think that he actually understood things like that.

Eloy spotted Spook in the snack bar. He went inside to see him.

Spook was eating a double-meat, double-everything cheeseburger with a double order of fries and onion rings and was drinking a beer.

The front of his shirt had an arrow pointing to his face, and underneath the arrow it read, THE MAN. Below that, it read, THE LEGEND, and below that was an arrow pointing toward his crotch.

Stan Buck was sitting at the same table and having his lunch: Coors Light. Stan Buck greeted Eloy in his usual fashion. "Hey, E, what the fuck? Over."

That meant, "How are you doing?"

"Hey, Stan," replied Eloy as he shook Stan's hand.

Eloy looked to Spook. "Looks like you're trying to rival Budde on who can eat the largest cheeseburger."

Spook shot Eloy the finger; he couldn't talk with his mouth so full.

"How the hell are you going to play golf after eating all that?"

Stan Buck retorted, "Hell, Eloy, cain't nothing fuck up Spook's game. He could eat a bowl of cement mix and follow it with water, and it wudn't bother his game at all." Stan laughed heartily at his own joke.

"Yeah," chipped in Bonner as he walked up to the table, "you got to have a game first in order to screw it up."

They were all greeted with another finger from Spook.

"Tell me, Stan, how are things going?" asked Eloy.

"They be fine."

"I didn't think you were ever going to come back to this 'fucking dirt-pile goat ranch' again, to use your own words."

"Aw, shit Eloy. I've been meaning to call you. I'm in the process of moving back to Odessa. Going to go back and work for my old company again. They ain't got nobody that can sell anything. They couldn't sell shit to flies. So Spook called me when he heard I was moving back, and I figured I could stop by on the way and suffer some more misery."

"Amarillo is kind of out of the way from Baton Rouge to Odessa, isn't it? Or did you just need the misery?"

"Naw, I'm just here doing Spook a favor. He gave me some song and dance about how he was playing good at the time and that if something went wrong he had an instant cure."

"Fell for that shit again, huh?"

"Hell, yeah. Hooked me and reeled me in." Stan made a motion like someone throwing a line into the water and then reeling it in. "Said he had some old girl we could bounce on like a trampoline. Hell, you know, Eloy, I ain't ever seen nothin' like a trampoline woman before. I've been to two or three hundred county fairs and several wagon wheel greasings, and I ain't ever seen a trampoline fuck before. Figured it was worth the trip just to watch the Spooker

T pole vault. I gotta call Benny Jaymen so he can watch too, in case he might want to add it to the fancy fuck."

"That might be hard to add, since I never seen a trampoline in anyone's bedroom," said Bonner.

"Oh, that part is always outside," said Spook, swallowing the last bite of his french fries.

Stan turned up his can of Coors Light and drank it to the bottom. While he was finishing that can, he was busy with his free hand reaching into his cooler and grabbing the next can. Stan always had a cooler of Coors Light nearby, and when one can was finished, his belief was that another beer should hit his lips instantly. Finish one in one sip, start the new one on the next sip; left arm down with the old, right arm up with the new. Stan even took his beer to the bathroom with him and drank it while he relieved himself. He could be heard to say, "Out with the old, in with the new."

Spook often called Stan "The Chemist." He could turn beer into piss. One of the crew told Stan if he could learn to suck his own dick, he could save a lot of money. Just recycle it.

"I can suck my own dick," replied Stan. "I just can't figure out how to get it to come out cold!"

"Spook must be paying for the misery and the entry fee," said Eloy, continuing the conversation.

"There you go," said Stan. "Might as well suffer with someone you like instead of an ex-wife . . . or worse."

"Ain't nothing worse. Ex-wives are the bottom of the barrel," said Spook. "Besides, piss on golf. I hate the fucking game!" Suddenly a glass-eyed look came on his face and he stared off into space. "But I can't leave it alone."

"As Bonner says, it's a game you love to hate," added Stan.

"Yeah," said Bonner, "if you look in *Funk & Wagnalls* dictionary under *golf*, it defines it as the most frustrating sport you'll ever love to hate. No shit! Golf spelled backward is *flog*, and that's what most people do."

"Since you hate golf now, Spook, does that mean we're bouncin' tonight?" asked Stan.

Spook didn't have time to answer Stan. Eloy butted in. "You know, Spook, off the golf course, you're a damn genius. You're just like that guy Richard Pryor talked about. You can book the numbers and don't even need paper or pencil. But as soon as you put on cleats, you stupid up. What the hell's with that?"

"I got the answer," said Bonner. "You see, them metal spikes act like grounding agents, just like a lightning rod, like fucking magnets, and when he puts his golf shoes on, they drain all the blood out of the boy's fucking brain. Just like his dick does when it hardens up. He's totally senseless. Can't think either way."

"Why don't you play in tennis shoes, Spook? Or maybe some of those Foot Joy teaching shoes?" asked Eloy.

"I've played in tennis shoes before."

"Well, did you play better?" asked Eloy.

"Well, he did think better. I don't know if he played better," replied Bonner, laughing.

"Yeah, I did better. And fuck you, Bonner. I just like wearing cleats better, that's all."

"Well, correct me if I'm wrong. But if I could play better, hell I'd wear goddamn high heels," said Eloy.

"And a fucking dress too," pitched in The Chemist.

"The problem is I just like the sound cleats make when you walk on cee-ment," answered Spook sheepishly.

"You play golf on grass, Spook, or have you forgot?" asked Eloy.

"Fuck you too," said Spook. "I just like the sound they make. Don't care nothing about them on the golf course. Hell, sometimes I even put 'em on in the morning when I go out and get the paper, just to hear the sound."

Everyone started laughing like hell.

"Why you don't you just put 'em on and walk up and down the street if it gives you a woody like that?" said Eloy.

"Why don't you just tape it and listen to it every day?" said Stan.

"I already tried that. Taping the sound just ain't the same," answered Spook with a strange, twisted look on his face. "It's like taping the sound of a climax. It's way better when it's in real time. Besides, I got to feel the crunch too."

"Why don't you wear 'em from the car to the pro shop and then put on your tennis shoes to play, then wear 'em from the pro shop back to your car, then you get the best of both worlds. Listen to the crunch and play better too," said Eloy.

"Too much fucking trouble, carrying two pairs of shoes. Besides, if I did, you three assholes wouldn't have nothing to rag my ass about anymore," said Spook. "Plus I still get the pleasure from the cleats on the cart paths."

"Yeah," said Bonner. "I bet between the three of us we could come up with a few subjects. You think, Eloy?"

"More than Edison has inventions." Eloy put his arm around Spook's shoulder. "Spook, you already carry around two pairs of shoes, just reverse the order in how you wear them."

A strange look came over Spook's face, like he had discovered uranium, or something else important.

Eloy said, "Somewhere, surely somewhere, in this vast world of ours, a village is being deprived of its idiot." Then he left his chair at the table to find the men's room.

"He's a fucking mental midget, E," said Bonner.

While Eloy was gone, Cassie came in and sat down at the table.

"So are you and Eloy getting everything all patched up?" asked Bonner as he motioned for the waitress to bring him and Cassie a beer. He didn't know where the regular waitress was; she wouldn't have let his beer get empty. He could only guess that this substitute didn't like people to drink.

"Patched up again, for good I hope this time. He seems more like the old Eloy to me. You know, Bonner, I didn't know if it was me or if the spark left or what. What really makes him tick?"

"Well, I guess I can explain it to you. But, Cassie, I can't understand it for you."

Cassie raised her eyebrows.

"Each of us are made up of the things we hate and more importantly the things we love. Eloy really loves playing the barbeque circuit, these two-man partnerships, hanging out with his friends, holding court, you know, telling lies, talking bullshit, being with a pretty lady and throwing money around, devil may care, like the amount is of no never mind to him. Now that's Eloy. That's what makes him tick. That's when he is the Eloy, not famous, notorious, Eloy Baines, The Breeze. Without all that, you take the E out of Eloy and destroy a very unique individual character. I hope that explains it some." Bonner looked at Cassie with a blank look on his face. "I don't even know if I understand what the fuck I just said, do you?"

Cassie laughed. It was actually the most intelligent thing she had ever heard any of them say, let alone Bonner Bennet. She took a sip of her beer. Beer really wasn't to her taste, so it wasn't a very big sip. "I guess that would about cover it. You know when he was in Tennessee, the longer he stayed, the more he changed. Slowly, he became a different person. He wasn't the same person I fell in love with. I shouldn't say this out loud, but he lost some of his snap."

Bonner got a shocked look on this face.

He turned in his chair and looked all around the bar to see who else had heard that comment and to see if Eloy was on his way back from the restroom.

"Damn, Cassie, don't say that too loud. Saying something like that is like saying a guy has a small dick."

"Well, you all do, don't you?"

"Maybe, but when a woman says it out loud, even if she's just funnin', it's like a confirmation. Guys just don't look at you the same anymore."

"I'll try to be more careful."

"He did tell me he was different up there," said Bonner.

"So he talked to you about it? Really? I don't believe it. What did he say?"

"He said, 'You know, Bonner, how things are always bigger in Texas. Well, the longer I stayed in Tennessee, the shorter my dick got. And hell, I ain't got that much too lose!"

Bonner gave Cassie a mischievous grin and then laughed like hell.

"That sounds just like him. I'm glad he's got his sense of humor back."

"Yep, I think the boy is gonna be okay."

"I believe so. He's back to writing again. So what is with this The Breeze thing?"

"It's Eloy's new nickname, his alter ego. You know as well as I do he's just like the breeze. Come and go as he pleases, go anywhere he wants, any time he wants, and there is nothing anyone can do about it."

"There you go. And you know I'd rather be in his world, here, than be in my world without him."

Triple J and Sunshine Ray agreed to play Bonner and Eloy, if they would both take Spook and Stan as a partner.

Triple J and Sunshine Ray figured if they did happen to lose the bet to Bonner and Eloy, they could win the money back on the bets against Spook and Stan. They were thinking that Spook and Stan wouldn't be able to help Bonner and Eloy enough to matter.

You know, it wasn't right what happened to Triple J and Sunshine Ray. Their strategy was sound, but they never counted on Spook being the Spook and doing the things he did to them. It was strange, eerie. It was almost unnatural."

Eloy had only seen Spook do these things when he played against Triple J. That was why he and Bonner gave him the moniker. He did things that just weren't natural, spooky things.

Stan Buck's bets stood all even going to the ninth hole. He had helped both Eloy and Bonner on two of holes to keep things square. Eloy and Bonner were up one bet in their match. Eloy and Spook were two bets down, going into the ninth hole. Bonner and Spook were also two bets down.

Spook stood to lose forty dollars. Not a large sum of money but significant to him. To him it actually meant he wouldn't be able to go to Stumpy's for two or three nights. Now that was a lot to lose. The chance of having to spend two or three nights at home, sober, with your wife—it was almost too much for him to bear. Or as it was in Spook's case, not with your wife, but not with the trampoline lady either. Both parties in the trampoline competition needed inhibition—enablers to get the mood right—and that required money. So two or three night at home watching *Wheel of Fortune* reruns was a nightmare for him.

Spook was the first to hit his second shot to the green from the ninth fairway. He semi bladed his nine-iron approach shot.

He was yelling, "Bite!" as he watched it sail over the green. "Bite, you skulled, money-losing motherfucker! Bite!" Spook yelled at the top of his lungs.

Located some forty yards beyond the ninth green was a red fire hydrant.

To the disbelief of Triple J and Sunshine Ray, and everyone else, the ball hit the fire hydrant flush. The ball ricocheted up and then backward and flew straight toward the green. It landed on the collar of the green, almost came to a stop, but then gently rolled down the incline. All of them watched incredulously as the ball rolled into the hole for an eagle two.

Eloy turned to Bonner and grinned. "Kiss a pussy," he said.

Bonner didn't hear him. Bonner was yelling, "Yeah, baby! Yeah, baby! Spook their fucking ass, baby!"

"Spooky muthafucka. I just hope he don't look at us too hard and catch us on fire or sumthin'," said Triple J as he threw his club to the ground.

"He be right paranormal, that boy be. 'Specially when he's pickin' on us my-nor-i-tees," said Sunshine.

Sunshine Ray went to his bag, got his gun, and put it in his belt. "I be ready iffin' he do's it again."

"Another shot like that and I'm gonna go get my gun too," said Triple J. "A knifing just wouldn't be good enough for his ass!"

Triple J and Sunshine Ray were so shook up they both bogeyed the ninth hole, allowing Bonner and Stan, Bonner and Eloy, and Eloy and Stan, to each win one bet. Bonner and Eloy won two bets.

The bet was doubled on the back nine. When they reached the eighteenth hole, the bets were reversed from what they had been on front nine. Stan's two teams were 4-2-0 each. Being 4-2-0 meant they were four holes up on the original bet, two holes up on the first press bet, and even on the second press bet. Bonner and Eloy were

3-1 on their bets. Eloy and Spook were 3-1 on their bet. Bonner and Spook were 3-1 on their bet.

Triple J and Sunshine Ray doubled the bet again so they could get even for the day if they won the hole.

The eighteenth hole was a slightly uphill, dogleg-right par-five.

Spook was the first to play. He swung extra hard and made his patented lunge toward the ball. He pull hooked his drive to the left of the trees that lined the fairway. His ball landed near a small building.

The small building was one of the golf course maintenance buildings. This particular building contained the master water control system for both courses. All of the switches and water control valves for the thirty-six holes at Ross Rogers were located in this one building.

The water control switches were small rubber tubes filled with water and controlled the valves to the main water lines for each fairway and green. The pressure of the water in the small rubber tubes controlled whether or not the valves were opened or closed. If the tubes were full of water, the valves remained closed. When the water was drained from the tubes, the valves would open and supply water to either the fairway sprinklers or the greens sprinklers. Each valve controlled a different set of sprinklers. As fate had it, the door to the shed was open. That was a grand mistake by the maintenance crew.

Spook found his tee ball near the shed. The ball lay in a sandy area with a clump of buffalo grass directly behind it, making it almost impossible to hit the shot forward. The smart play would have been for Spook to play the ball sideways back to the fairway and then have a good approach to the green. But Spook had on his spikes—so smart wasn't one of the options.

Bonner got Eloy's attention. "Watch this shit. He's going to try to hit it, the dumb sum-bitch. And no matter what we say, we can't ever talk him out of it. Think you could hit that?"

"Not this white man. That's harder than trying to put socks on a chicken."

"That's hard, ain't it?"

"Must be. Ever seen any socks on any chicken?"

"Nope, can't say as I have."

"Case closed!"

Spook chose his three iron and took a mighty swing. The buffalo grass moved four feet; the ball moved only three feet.

Spook looked at the ball and knew instantly that he had played the wrong shot and that it might possibly cost him winning his bets—plus the ridicule from Bonner and Eloy about being stupid with his spikes on.

Here he was, finally going to get to beat Triple J out of some money, and he went stupid again. Spook got this scrunched, evil look on his face, a look one might get if they were trying to shit four strands of barbed wire.

In a fit of rage, Spook slung the three iron as hard as he could. He hung onto the handle too long and when it left his hand, its direction was in a straight line with the master water control building. The building with the open door, the building with all those rubber tubes filled with water.

The three iron hit the doorframe, breaking the club into two pieces. The grip end of the club fell to the ground. The heaviest piece, the three-iron head with part of the broken shaft attached, flew into the building. The broken shaft acted like a straight razor, whirling around like a helicopter blade, shearing the water-filled small rubber tubes in half. That was how the valves worked: keep water pressure on them and they were closed. Remove the water pressure and the valves would open.

When the broken three iron severed the rubber tubes, instantly sprinkler heads all across the golf course started rising out of their resting places and began to spray all of the unsuspecting golfers with gallons of water.

Spook then realized what he had done. The look on his face switched from one of shitting four strands of barbed wire to one of sheer terror. Quickly, Spook ran to the shed and grabbed both pieces of the broken three iron.

He jumped into his golf cart and drove over to the next fairway so anyone seeing him head for the clubhouse would think he was playing a different hole other than the eighteenth hole, and then he drove to the cart barn.

All of the others quickly followed and left Ross Rogers as fast as they could. All bets were called even. They all went to Triple J's nightclub to hide.

Spook blamed the accident on Dude, the Ross Rogers greens superintendent. In Spook's own words, "If Dude would have closed that fucking door, then none of that would have happened, dumb fucker. We would have probably won the bets too. Cost me a hundred forty dollars."

Spook cry-babied Triple J into buying him a beer.

Triple J owned a nightclub just a block north of Amarillo Boulevard on North Hughes Street called The E-Z Inn.

He said he called it that because people liked to ease on in, then ease on out. No one just walked in or walked out of The E-Z Inn. They eased.

It was an after-hours lounge and most people, Eloy discovered, just eased on out the back door, after they had eased on in the front door. It was mostly an afterhours bar for blacks, and every once in a while, some whites would show up. As long as Triple J was there, there was never any trouble. Eloy always felt lucky when he got to go to The E-Z Inn, and he felt even luckier when he got to leave.

One of the biggest sellers in The E-Z Inn was the catfish sandwich. The regular customers would order a whole, fried catfish between two pieces of bread. They could eat the bread and the meat of the catfish, leaving only the bone.

It was one of the most amazing things Eloy had ever seen. Every time he tried it, he ended up in the emergency room with catfish bones stuck in his throat.

The E-Z Inn was one of those places where, out in the parking lot, you could buy absolutely anything you could dream up or ever desire. You could buy a car, a woman, a hit man, and all variations of dope. Hell, you could even buy collard greens.

There was one thing Eloy had never figured out. It was finally made plain to him that night at The E-Z Inn. No matter where Bonner went or what he did, no one ever messed with Bonner, never caused him one bit of trouble. They might get mad as hell, but they wouldn't do anything like try to fight or something. Nope, they never touched one single hair on his head.

Bonner always dressed in a flashy manner. This particular day, he wore bright-red slacks, a white shirt with some red trim on the collar and sleeves, and white patent-leather shoes.

If Eloy, Spook, or any of the others ever dressed that brightly, they would probably go home with two black eyes—but no one messed with Bonner. It was explained by the man sitting on the bar stool next to Eloy.

"Boy, dat B-Man be some flashy somethin', huh?" the man said as Bonner walked by.

That comment was something coming from a man wearing a satin shirt and black patent-leather shoes with pointed toes covered with gold.

"Yeah, no shit. If I ever dressed like that, I'd probably get stabbed and left out back in the Dumpster."

"Yeah, less you was going to one of them swissy-tail joints up on the Boulevard, or pimpin'. But nobody mess wiff the B-Man."

"Why is that? All the years I've known him, I haven't figured it out. Nobody ever fucks with him. How come?"

"Well, uh, see, uh," the man looked to his left and then to his right to see if anyone else was listening. "The B-Man be knowin', uh, peoples who, uh, you know, peoples who, uh, do bad things, uh, to other peoples. In the army, he was one of them coverts peoples, you know behind enemy lines, sneaking around doing shit shouldn't be mentioned."

Eloy wondered who spread that complete fabrication. In the army, Captain Bonner Bennet was in charge of sports and recreation. It was a perfect example of it's not what you do that matters, it is what people *think* you do.

"See where I'm comin' from, E? I mean if anyone mess wiff the B-Man, they end up kilt or worse. Mess wiff him, shit, next day, wake up deader than a muthafucker. And all your shit be gone too. They never find it neither, no lawd. Car gone, wallet gone, all you'ins household shit, *poof!* Fucking gone. Ain't magic neither, and your body is all grount up wid some pig sausage over to the east side. No funeral, zip. Just like you was vaporized and never existed."

Eloy was intrigued. He smiled slightly and took a sip of his Dewar's as the man continued.

The man gave Eloy a stern look. "Be lucky he likes your white ass. You know, peoples that mess with peoples for a living don't even fuck with the B-Man, shit no. He connects like a sink to a pipe. Mess wiff him and down you go. That pipe don't go nowhere no good."

"Yeah I know. We were in the same unit in the army, coverts and shit," lied Eloy.

On hearing that the man's head snapped around and he said with a quiver in his voice, "Shit man, sorry I said anything. I should sit somewhere else."

The next afternoon, they finished their last practice round before the tournament began. Eloy and Bonner joined Spook and Stan at the long bar in Stumpy's. They ordered drinks and sat next to them at the bar.

As they sat down, Spook looked at Eloy, with the same strange look he had had the previous day on his face. He said in a monotone voice, "It won't work, will it, Stan?"

"What's that?"

"Wearing the spikes from the car to the pro shop and then changing into tennis shoes."

"Won't work," said Stan, The Chemist, talking and sipping a Coors Light at the same time.

"Why won't it work?" asked Eloy. He wanted to hear this explanation.

"It's the cart paths. They're by the tee boxes and the greens. When you get out on the cart paths, you get to feel and hear the crunch of the spikes on the concrete. You get to hear it all the time. Just gives off the satisfaction, lasts for four, five hours."

"So did you think of that, Spook, or did Stan?" asked Bonner.

"It kinda came to us simultaneously. Had to mull it over with a couple of beers, then it came to me. If they had golf courses without cart paths, it might work; otherwise, no way, Jose. Only place I know without cart parts is Clayton, New Mexico, and I ain't moving there."

Eloy looked at the two and realized it was beer thirty. Even though it was just past four o'clock, it was beer thirty. *Beer thirty* was the time of day when Stan or Spook, or anyone else for that matter, had consumed enough alcohol that their IQ went up to the stratosphere. They simply became smarter than they were before—hell, smarter than everyone. All the world's puzzles became plain. They could decipher military secrets, cure incurable diseases, and even talk to each other in Morse code and understand what each was saying.

Hell, Spook once worked a Rubik's Cube with only one hand.

Stan once recited the formula for making TNT.

"So all that Coors Light you boys been drinking helped you figure that out?" said Eloy.

"Yep, it's like this. If it wasn't for Coors Brewing Company, we'd all be speaking Japanese today," said Stan.

"Or maybe Russian," added Spook.

"Boy, I bet the explanation for this is gonna be a lulu!" exclaimed Bonner.

"Now what the hell does Coors have to do with the Japanese?" asked Eloy.

"As smart as you are, Eloy, with all that ed-u-ma-cation you got, I can't believe you don't know this. Maybe your poor old hardworking mama wasted her money on that tuition," replied Stan. "Back when we was fighting Japan and was trying to figure out how to make the atom bomb, the scientists worked and worked and worked but were stuck, just couldn't figure it out, couldn't figure how to make the bomb blow up just right."

"Oh, they thought they knew how to explode it all right, but it couldn't explode just any old place or any old way. You know, fuck up a test run and *poof!* There goes all the help," interjected Spook.

"Yeah, the work hours were long and stressful. Right then and there, the government invented happy hour. Believe that? Fucking government invented happy hour."

Stan and Spooked laughed.

Eloy and Bonner grinned.

"So," Stan continued, "the government sent them some Coors Light, they took a break, drank a twelve pack, and *bam!* Fusion solved, fucking atom bomb. So long, Nagasaki."

"You mean Hiroshima."

"Yeah, we got them too. Hell of an explosion!"

"Coors Light wasn't even a product back then, you dumb shits," said Bonner.

Spook smiled real big and countered, "You're the dumb shit, 'cause all you know is golf. You ain't real smart 'bout nuthin' else. Know of any smart people that would wear red britches?"

Spook waited for an answer from Bonner. All he got was the finger.

"See, Coors Light wasn't for the public back then. It was a still a government experiment to see if drinking the right mix of alcohol was good for the brain. Coors just happened to figure it out. They named it Coors Light for one, because it was not as heavy as the old Coors, and two, if you drank the right mixture, *click! Flash!* On went the Intelligence Light." He snapped his fingers to emphasize his point. "See, dumb ass? Coors Light."

Eloy looked to Bonner.

Bonner looked to Eloy.

Eloy looked to Samantha, the bartender.

She rolled her eyes and looked to the heavens.

"It was first made way back when," said Stan. "They had it way back in the early 1900s but couldn't sell it. All them miners wanted something more substantial than a nonheavy beer. If they had known of the side effects, they probably could've found more gold and silver than they did—they would have found it faster anyways. Or maybe one or two of them could have become doctors or something and wouldn't have died from that shovel disease. Coors had the government run some test and now you have the Paul Harvey."

"So do other alcohols work, or is it only Coors Light?" asked Eloy.

"Hell, E, take a look at the Japanese," said Spook. "They were drinking that foul-tasting sake. Do you know how it's made? From rice. And they use them water buffalo to help cultivate that rice. So all that rice soaks up all that water buffalo shit, and that's what makes it taste so bad." He made a face that looked like he had just tasted a turd.

"And look at where drinking sake got them," he continued. "All they wanted to do was get a knife and chop up shit, and wear them funny-looking robes with a headscarf tied around the waist. They was playing with knifes and doing that Ginsu stuff and we was playing with bombs. Which side of that bet you want?"

"You smart ones know that Coors is made by a guy named Adolf, don't you?"

"Yeah, but it ain't Hitler. They was cousins, and when Hitler got smoked by Patton, Adolf Coors hightailed it out of Europe and came here and made friends. That's why he picked Colorado, 'cause it was cold and shit just like home."

"Really?"

"Yep, he made vodka back in Russia but switched to beer when he got here. He had finally figured out vodka only makes you stupid. Look at what happened to them aliens," said Stan, talking and drinking at the same time. He could talk out of one side of his mouth and pour beer down the other side, and you could still understand what he was saying.

"Aliens?" said Samantha.

"Yep, aliens. See . . . It's been kept secret, but the first aliens landed in Russia back in 1938. The rooskies took 'em in and befriended them and taught 'em how to drink vodka. Then when they was all friendly and all, they convinced 'em to come over here to attack us with their beva-watt-laser-click ray guns and them drunk sum-bitches fucked it up. You know one hit from that beva-watt-laser-click and you could look down at the hole in your chest and see where you'd been—then *frizzt!* You'd melt like ice in July. So why do you think them aliens crashed at Roswell instead of at White Sands or Albuquerque?"

"Or even Dallas? I mean shit." Spook was trying hard to keep from laughing. "They flew right past New York City and Omaha."

"'Cause," Stan continued, "they was drunk on vodka, totally fucked up the invasion! Dumb-assed rooskies forgot to cut 'em off the happy juice till the job was done."

"Dumb fuckin' rooskies," said Spook, opening another Coors Light.

Stan continued. "So when the lead pilot handed his glass of vodka to his copilot and said, 'Now watch this shit,' he crashed and burned. He was the one they found. Now the rest of them little fuckers knew if the lead pilot couldn't fly drunk, they didn't have a chance in hell of doing it, so they flew off and were never found or heard from again, beva-watt-laser-click ray guns and all." Then Stan smiled like he was a student in a class and had just given the correct answer to the teacher's question.

"And that's what started the Bermuda Triangle," Spook said. "And that's the fucking truth." With that statement, he finished his current Coors Light and opened another can of pure genius.

"They originally were gonna call it the Vodka Triangle, but it sounded too much like a couple of chicks and some lucky guy were just getting it on. So they changed the name not to confuse those people who don't drink Coors Light."

"What about scotch? Eloy drinks scotch and he's kind of smart," said Samantha.

"Hell, you ever see Eloy do anything smart when he's got a snoot full. I mean look at him now and who he's hanging out with, dumb ass. Hell, if Eloy drank Coors Light, he might write better songs than he does. Dumb fuck even jumped out of a perfectly flying airplane once."

"Is that right?" asked Samantha, raising her eyebrows.

"Actually, it was more than once, but for different reasons," said Bonner, replying for Eloy.

"See, I told you he did, a perfectly flying airplane, and boop, out the door goes old scotch-smart Eloy," said Stan.

"I'm sure there must have been one Coors Light drinker onboard," someone said.

"Sure there was. Someone had to tell Eloy to put on his chute, didn't he? Eloy wouldn't have thought of it by his own self. He would a jumped out the door chute-less and splaaaat. Ah, look, Eloy's now a pancake. But the Coors Light boy didn't jump."

"Why's that?" asked Eloy.

"See? See what a dumb ass he is? Someone had to fly the plane now, didn't they?" said Spook.

"I know one thing," continued Stan, "he'd damn sure putt better if he was on Coors Light. Scotch only makes you jickey. I tried scotch once and had nine three putts in eight holes."

Now there is a true beer thirty comment, thought Eloy.

Bonner said, "Nine three putts in eight holes. I once had nine putts in eight holes."

Samantha asked another question. "So if Bonner here put down his Miller Lite and had a Coors Light, you're telling me he'd get smarter, right?"

"Well, it is more complicated than that. See, guys that drink Miller Light would have to be real careful, be weaned off the Miller before the Coors could take effect. Might take a month or so. Doing it too fast might cause some neurological damage, screw up their brain, then they'd just run around with their zippers down, slobbering everywhere." Spook started laughing as he talked. When he stopped laughing, he continued. "Then Eloy here, he can't convert at all. Scotch drinkers are doomed to a life of nonenlightenment. See, scotch kills the neuromic cell receptors in the brain. Without the neuromic receptors, the Coors Light can't work."

"Are you talking about the neuronal membrane?" Eloy asked.

"See there?" said Stan. "He cain't even pronounce it right, so I know he don't even know about the neuromics of the brain. See, under a microscope, they look like little tiny ladles. You gotta have the receptors so when you drink the right amount of Coors Light the neuromics of the brain become full and excited and the gray matter reaches the perfect consistency for paranormal thinking."

Eloy started laughing at the absurdity of it all.

Spook's eyes glazed over like he was in a trance. "Hell, folks, me and The Chemist have even figured out how to cure world hunger."

"Yep, damn sure did!" chimed in Stan, raising his can of Coors Light in a salute.

"Okay, I'll bite," Samantha said, knowing she probably shouldn't have said it. "How do you cure world hunger?"

Simultaneously, Spook and Stan said, "Fuck man, *feed* 'em!"

Then they both broke out in raucous laughter, slapping hands and banging on the bar counter top.

"Case closed," said Stan, finally able to talk again. "Now you boys who've been to college and all, figure it out."

Bonner spoke up. "Since we're on all of this extrasensory, intellectual intercourse, I have a mystery."

"Wait a second. I don't see no one doing no intercourse," said Stan.

"Not sexual intercourse, dumb ass, conversational intercourse," said Samantha.

"What he really means, Stan, is that he's not physically fucking you, he's fucking you mentally," added Eloy.

"Oh, got it."

"Anyway," Bonner continued, "I'm trying to figure out why we tip like we do. I mean if Samantha makes six trips to bring us six beers, we only tip her a dollar or two. But if she makes one trip and brings us a bottle of champagne or something expensive, then we tip her more, and then we even have to serve ourselves. Don't make sense to me. How about you guys?"

"You must have been drinking Coors Light to think of that," said Spook. "It only makes sense to me."

"So we tip by the trip? Same tip for a hamburger or a steak?" said Eloy.

"Yep, the same. From now on boys, tip by the trip. Minimum one dollar for the first trip, then fifty cents a trip thereafter."

"Yippee," said Samantha. "I'm getting a raise!"

Suddenly, sunshine filled the room as the back door of Stumpy's opened and Cassie stood in the doorway.

Eloy wondered why it was always the back door of all of these joints that everyone used. He decided that if he ever saw anyone come in the front door, he was diving for cover. He had asked Bonner about it, and Bonner told him he was right.

Bonner said he and Spook were in the Sixteenth Avenue Lounge one day and this great big old boy came in through the front door. He said before it was all said and done, the great big old boy beat the cornbread shit out of everyone in there except for him and Spook. Then just like he came in, he left, out the front door. It was the only time they had ever seen anyone come and go by the front door. He said as the fight was happening they stood by the back door and watched so they could have made a good getaway if he happened to approach them. He said that's when they started coming to Stumpy's. Any bar that allowed that to happen must be in a bad neighborhood.

Cassie stood for a moment letting her eyes adjust to the dimness of the room.

The bartender, Samantha, asked, "Could I help you, ma'am?"

Cassie spotted Eloy, Bonner, Stan, and Spook sitting on the stools on the other side of the bar. She nodded their way and said, "I'm just looking for Huey, Dewey, and Louie there."

Samantha said, "Them? You really looking for them? Guess you don't drink Coors Light, do you?"

Cassie gave Samantha a puzzled look.

"It's a long story, but you missed the invention of Coors Light and how it saved us from saying, 'Domo Arigato,' all the time. By the way, Goofy is with them too."

"Which one is Goofy?"

"You pick it."

Cassie ordered a vodka and soda with lemon.

"You ever get tired of these boys and their BS?" asked Cassie.

"If they didn't tip as well as they do, I wouldn't even let 'em in door. Besides, it would be just like trying to herd cats. You know, dear, all men are animals. Some just make better pets. Be careful over there. They are in their enlightenment period."

"Beer thirty, huh?"

Cassie walked up behind Eloy just in time to hear Spook say, "I ain't ever ate any pussy, but I have been fed some."

"Yeah, you wish," Cassie said as she looked at him and rolled her eyes. "Ah, look what I found, a row of fools on a row of stools."

All of them turned to look.

Eloy stood up, put his arm around Cassie's waist, and gave her a hug and a quick kiss.

She was wearing Wranglers, boots, and a white, sleeveless western shirt. She smelled like one of those French pastry things you could put in your mouth and it would melt instantly on contact with your tongue. She rivaled Adie Connors in that department.

"Damn!" Eloy said. "You smell good enough to eat."

Then Eloy rolled his eyes back in his head, turned up his lip, and snorted like a bull does when he gets around a cow in her season.

Cassie didn't seem impressed. She hit him in the back of the head.

She looked at the drink sitting in front of Eloy. It wasn't his usual Dewar's and water, hold the water. It was a tall glass of light red liquid.

"Funny-looking color for Dewar's?" she inquired pointing at Eloy's glass.

"It's a cerveza Mexicana rojo," Eloy said, taking a drink.

"And that would be?"

Samantha answered, "Beer, tomato juice, and a shot of tequila."

"Wonderful. How many have you had?"

Eloy responded, "Couple or so."

Samantha raised her left hand with all five fingers extended and her right hand with one finger raised.

"Good job, Eloy," said Cassie. "You know what beer does to you. And I have better things in mind than watching you sleep."

"It's okay, hon. I was just trying to get as smart as Spook and The Chemist. Plus it puts lead in your pencil."

"Plus you still ain't smart."

"I heard it was only unleaded anyway," interjected Samantha.

Eloy gave them both the finger.

Stan said, "Eloy, me and Spook got a new song for you. We wanted to wait 'till Cassie was here in case she wants to use it at the rodeo. Here goes." Stan spoke the words. His singing voice sounded like someone drowning in a deep well. "I got a girlfriend named Twalla. Twalla likes to walla. It cost two dollars to walla with Twalla. A dolla more to have her swalla."

Stan guffawed. So did Spook.

Samantha said, "Good god almighty!"

"What do you think?"

"For a dollar, huh," said Cassie. "And to think all this time I've been doing it for free."

"Are you looking for anyone in particular, or you wantin' to handle all of us?" said Spook.

Cassie walked over and gave Spook a light kiss on the cheek and said, "Spooker T, you shouldn't cast a pearl before swine."

"Hey, Eloy, 'fore you leave, me and Spook got us a new venture and we need us an investor," said Stan.

Eloy waited for him to continue.

"Yeah, see, we have come up with a new douche powder fragrance and we need some seed money."

"Don't you just love beer thirty?" said Bonner.

"So what's wrong with the ones they have now? You got something better than strawberry, rose, or pina colada?" said Samantha.

"Oh hell, yeah. The greatest smell of all time: new-car smell."

"You teasing, right?" said Cassie.

"Nope, everyone I ever knowed who bought a new car always said the same thing. Good god o-mighty, don't you just love how a new car smells. Every one of them, man, woman or child says it. Be the best douche powder of all times."

"Well you're right about that."

"We also be thinking about barbeque."

"Apple wood or mesquite?" said Eloy.

"New Car might work," said Cassie.

"But barbeque won't," interrupted Samantha, "nope, won't work."

"She's right," said Cassie. "Once you boys got a whiff of the barbeque smell then you'd be up and off to the kitchen looking for something to eat leaving us girls all hot and naked having to just to get romantic with ourselves. Then we might actually discover we don't need men anymore."

"Okay, that's it then, put the nix on the barbeque," said Stan.

"I can't do it," said Eloy, "All my money is tied up in a new alcohol formula. It contains all of the daily recommended vitamins right in the drink. Have a couple of pops and *BAM!* You're good for the day."

"See . . . he still ain't smart. Hell, Eloy, just take a handful of them vitamins and wash 'em down with a beer or two and you got the same thing."

"Better have a few more beers, you're getting' stupid. What if you forget your pills, or leave one out? This way you don't have to go to Walgreens all the time. Don't have to think about. Just stop in at your favorite watering hole, have a couple, and automatically get the daily dose of vitamin A, B, C, D, E, F, G, H, I, and K. Plus all of them valuable minerals: calcium, magnesium, etcetera. You could have birth control in one, and in another some drug that would help your unit get hard after you had drank too much. How's that for a scotch drinker?"

"Reckon there is hope for you yet," spoke The Chemist.

Cassie turned to Eloy. She certainly didn't want to spend her afternoon listening to the same old war stories embellished in a new and different way and listening to the same old lies. And she certainly didn't want to stay long enough for her clothes to smell like an ashtray. She whispered in his ear, "Care for a lewd encounter?"

Eloy nodded his head yes.

Cassie leaned close to Eloy's ear. In her sexiest whisper, Cassie said, "Do you know how fast frozen whipped cream melts on a big hot hard-on?"

Eloy got off the stool and laid some money on the bar. He didn't finish his drink.

Spook said, "Eloy, you'd better finish that red beer. You know there are sober kids in China."

Eloy didn't laugh and didn't say a word. He was concentrating on Miss Whipped Cream America. As he walked to his car, he wondered if Carnation knew the actual melting point of whipped cream on a hard dick.

"You know she would go real well with a cold beer," said Stan.

"Even better with a pina colada," Samantha added.

Cassie cuddled up close to Eloy and said, "Damn, Eloy, you finally found it, didn't you?"

"Yeah," he said, grinning like a new pup on a fat teat. "Lewis and Clark didn't discover everything, now did they?"

"Well, I'm proud of you. Just don't forget where it is. Most men will spend twenty minutes looking for a lost golf ball but won't spend thirty seconds looking for a woman's G-spot."

"I'll tell you what, Cassie. That screw was so good your neighbors are probably having a cigarette right now."

Cassie laughed and asked Eloy, "Why do you think they call it 'screwing'? There isn't a screw motion in the whole process. It's more of a pumping action. Why don't they call it 'pumping' instead of 'screwing'?"

"The janitor at the savings and loan in Clovis does call it pumping, but he pronounces it poomphin'. Like, 'Have you poomphed old so and so lately?' Anyway, hell, don't ask me. There's a lot of stuff I haven't figured out yet."

"And that would be?"

"Why they don't use Velcro on men's pants instead of zippers?"

Cassie looked at him like he was a little boy asking some dumb question. Then she replied, "Probably 'cause they would make too much noise in the movie theater."

Eloy laughed hard. "There must be some history there, but I won't go there."

"Well, the question did remind me of the joke. The lady sitting in a movie theater tells her husband that the man in the seat next to her is masturbating. The husband says, disgustingly, 'Let's change seats.' She says they can't. He asks why. She says, 'Well, 'cause he's using my hand.'"

Eloy laughed again. "Is there history there too?"

Cassie just laughed.

"Tell me this. A woman will stick a cigarette in her mouth with no thought of consequence to her health, but most won't suck a dick. You know I never heard of anyone getting throat or lung cancer from sucking a dick. Have you? I think we need a government study. I could head it up."

"You may be worse than crazy, but you can catch diseases from oral sex."

Cassie got up, found the scotch in the bar, mixed them two drinks, and returned to the bedroom. "You know," said Cassie, "most of the guys you hang out with are as crazy as you. All of us come up with stuff that is insane or ludicrous."

"What's ludicrous?"

"See, see what I mean?"

"Well, you're too young for it, but all of us are all about the same age and when we were kids they used DDT to kill off mosquitoes."

"I've heard of DDT. It's a poison that was banned, right?"

"Yeah, and they banned it some years ago, bad for the environment and bad for humans. Anyway, when we were kids, like in grade school, these trucks would come down the alleys behind our houses and spray this huge cloud of DDT. Of course, being the smart little shits we were back then, we would run behind those trucks chasing them and inhaling all that DDT. Bonner said that was what did it, what caused our minds to warp, and he can't be wrong now, can he?"

Then he started singing. You couldn't really classify Eloy's voice as a singing voice. It sounded like a frog in heat sitting on a wet rock, but he was trying as hard as he could.

I always said I would take it any way I could,
But standing up wasn't all that good.
Now I don't know how this will really sound,
But I just take mine laying down.

Cassie sat the drinks on the nightstand and got back into bed. She knew where this was going. Eloy took a sip of his Dewar's and water, hold the water, and continued to sing.

> Now all bent over or sitting in a chair,
> Just never did much to really get me there.
> So just tell everybody, tell it all over town,
> Ole Eloy will just take his laying down.

He took another drink and finished the song.

> Now your evil thoughts, you can just keep.
> I'm just talking about trying to get some sleep.

Eloy laughed like hell and then said, "What happened to the Cool Whip on that first go-around?"

"That's for ride number two."

"Ride two? Damn, I didn't know this was a rodeo. Are we doing bull riding, saddle broncs, or the bareback thing?"

Cassie took a drink of the scotch and took an ice cube into her mouth. She stuck her head under the sheet and mumbled, "Definitely bareback."

Over coffee, Eloy told Cassie what had happened when Spook tried to flood the Ross Rogers golf course.

"You guys don't ever seem to learn, do you? That Neanderthal attitude never gets you anywhere."

"It isn't our fault actually," explained Eloy. "Van Gogh started it."

"Really? I didn't know they played golf back then."

"Why hell yeah," said Eloy grinning. "They even played back during Jesus's time. He was playing with the apostles once at the Dead Sea Country Club and Baptism Resort when it was overheard, 'Jesus, what a nice shot!'"

"Your brain is really soaked, isn't it? The DDT kicking in?"

Eloy shrugged his shoulders and grinned. "You should try alcohol and DDT sometime and see how you can function."

"I know better than to ask this, but just how *did* Van Gogh start the Neanderthal thing?"

"He was playing with his buddies one day and said, 'If I miss this putt, I'll cut off my fucking ear!'"

Thursday at the Ross Rogers was the qualifying round for teams wanting to play in the Championship Flight. Thirty-two teams competed. The best sixteen teams would be seeded, according to score, in the Championship Flight, and the next sixteen teams would be seeded into the President's Flight. No team wanted to be in the President's Flight. Everyone called it the Cry Baby Flight. Both scores of the two partners counted, so it was a tough format. No mistakes if you wanted to qualify.

Eloy laughed when he saw the names on the scoreboard: Bennet, Bonner, and Breeze, E.B.

R.T. and Spencer Wampler played and qualified fourth.

Eloy and Bonner qualified tenth due to Eloy making a double bogey on the par-three, seventeenth hole—again. The seventeenth hole was a medium-length par-three over water, 180 yards from the back tee. Eloy hit his first ball in the water and then proceeded to make his five. "I never have liked that hole," he commented. "Sets up bad for me."

Bonner said, "Maybe you ought to consider laying up, E. You know, hit a wedge short of the water, and then hit a wedge to the green. Least you could make a four, unless you three-putted."

Eloy laughed.

As usual, after the round was completed, they went to Stumpy's.

Cassie came in the back door just as Bonner was leaving.

"Where are you off to so early, Bonner?"

"I'm going home and make my wife the happiest woman in the whole world."

"Really," said Cassie. "Reckon she'll miss you all that much?"

Bonner laughed and gave her a high five.

Cassie sat down next to Eloy. "What are you Einsteins dissecting today?" she asked.

"Oh, we were just discussing the types of fucks there are. You know, like the pity fuck, the thank-you-I-needed-that, stuff like that. The newest being is the novelty fuck."

"A novelty?"

"Yeah, you see it's not like a sport fuck where someone's just banging as many and as often as they can. The novelty fuck is where, just every once in a while, you get some just for the fun of it. No romance, no kissing, none of that stuff. You know, just a quick little pop to relieve the tension. Hell, you don't even have to know their name."

Cassie said, "That sounds special. No kissing and hugging. Where do I sign up? It's certainly something I've always looked forward to."

"The sign-in sheet is right over here, darling," said Spook, grabbing his crotch.

"But you know, on second thought, you might have to rethink this one. Women can't do it without romance."

"Sure they can. They do it all the time. You just mean you won't," said Eloy.

"Won't, can't. There you go, finally making sense."

"I'll tell you one thing, if some broad came in here right now and said she needed help with a climax or two, one of these good old boys in here would certainly help her out. No discussion, no foreplay, nothing. Just jump up and *pow!* Right in the pussy."

"Hell, Eloy, that doesn't mean anything," said Cassie. "There is probably a good old boy in here who'd hump a wild animal if it walked in and was in heat."

"Cassie," said Spook, laughing, "you mean like a dog or something?"

"It was a chicken. Leave me alone," said Stan.

The whole bar erupted with laughter.

"So no dialogue or anything?" said Cassie, looking at Eloy.

He responded, "Oh there's dialogue. She says, 'I need some help.' He says, 'Okay.' Then they discuss whose car they're going to use or if they're just gonna go out behind the big tree behind the Sixteenth Avenue."

"Or perhaps just a quickie in the ladies room," Samantha chimed in.

Cassie looked at Eloy and batted her eyes. Then she grabbed his thigh and gave it a squeeze. "You know, I'm thinking I might need help with a climax or three."

"Romance, sport, or novelty?"

Cassie leaned over and kissed Eloy. "How 'bout all three?"

"See, what'd I tell you, Spook? Some broad would come in wantin' some help," said Eloy. "You lose, Samantha, drinks are on Spook."

"So are you volunteering or do I have to go public?"

"No, hell no. I'm in. Now what order do you want them in?"

"Let's see. Okay. How 'bout we combine them and have a new classification?"

"And that would be?"

"A mega fuck. Like a fancy fuck on steroids!"

Eloy grinned from ear to ear. "Yippee! One full Pompeii for The Breeze!"

"So are you going to sit here and run that mouth or are you going to take me somewhere where we can scream and yell and break up some furniture and you can show me this full Pompeii of yours?"

Friday at 8:00 a.m., Eloy and Bonner played their first match of the Ross Rogers tournament.

The Ross Rogers tournament was a match-play event with two points available, to win or lose, on each hole. The score of both players counted. There was one point for the low score on the hole and the other point was for the combined total of the two partners.

Bonner played good, carding a sixty-eight.

Eloy managed a respectable seventy and actually made par on his nonfavorite hole, the par-three seventeenth hole.

Even as good as they played, they were one point down coming into the par-five eighteenth.

And even though they both made birdie on the eighteenth hole, they lost the first match by one point.

Eloy had a putt for an eagle that would have tied the match. It curled around the hole and then stopped on the high side, but it didn't fall in.

So once again, along with his partner Bonner, Eloy was resigned to the consolation bracket. The "except for one putt bracket," Eloy called it.

They went to Stumpy's that afternoon to console themselves.

"Bonner, I don't know what we can do. That was pretty good playing today—especially by you."

"We both played good. But it's always the same when you lose a close match. It comes down to a putt or two."

Cassie came by before heading to the fairgrounds for her rodeo performance.

"Hey, Cassie," said Spook. "Did you come by to get a little to warm up that high note?"

"That's all you think about, isn't it? You guys are horny all the time."

"That's not really true. Not all the time. Only on days that start with a T," said Eloy.

"That's not many. Kind of leaves out the weekends though, doesn't it?" responded Cassie.

"Nah, not really. See I'm only horny on Tuesday, Thursday, Thanksgiving, Today, Tomorrow, Thaturday, and Thunday."

Spook showed up for Saturday's matches in a new dark-blue T-shirt. The front left chest area was embroidered with the letters DEA in bright gold.

When Eloy saw it, he thought it looked exactly like the shirt the narcotics officers wore. He wondered how in the world Spook ever talked anyone associated with the Drug Enforcement Agency into giving him an official shirt. He also wondered why Spook or Bonner would ever want to be associated with anyone in the

Drug Enforcement Agency. But then he reasoned it would be for protection.

The mystery was solved when Eloy saw the back of the shirt. The DEA read, DRUNK EVERY AFTERNOON. Eloy wasn't real smart, or he would have known Spook could have never gotten a real shirt.

Saturday was the day you had to play thirty-six holes, if you were fortunate enough to win your first match.

If you lost the first match, it was sayonara, so long, exit stage left from the Ross Rogers Partnership. Two losses at the Ross Rogers and you were out.

For their morning match, they drew the club champion from Tascosa Country Club and a doctor of some sort.

Eloy saw them on the driving range and knew instantly which one the doctor was—he had on the loudest, ugliest golf pants Eloy had ever seen. They were paisley or some pattern like that, and they were pink and purple. They looked like remnants from a tie factory. Any respectable club champion would never dress like that.

He confirmed his judgment when Sunshine Ray and Triple J looked at the doctor's pants and laughed.

The doctor's shirt was green and blue madras. You couldn't watch him swing. With all of the colors going every which way, it reminded Eloy of someone who was throwing up a pizza.

This doctor, of some sort, had a golf bag big enough to hold his clubs and a pony keg of beer, and maybe even a sleeping bag. It barely fit on the golf cart.

Bonner introduced Eloy to Dr. Van Hooten.

The match went back and forth with both teams playing well. Van Hooten played better than he dressed.

Each time Bonner would putt, he would have Van Hooten stand where he couldn't see him and his clothes.

Van Hooten said he thought Bonner was rude.

Bonner didn't care one way or the other.

Once, on a crucial putt, Van Hooten wouldn't move. So Eloy stood between him and Bonner so Bonner could make the putt.

This time, the two birdies they made on the eighteenth hole gave them a victory.

Eloy figured the doctor's clothes had been their downfall. How could you concentrate on golf having to look at that for four hours? Eloy and Bonner never saw Van Hooten hit a single shot during the match. They refused to watch him.

Their next match was due to begin at 2:00 p.m. It gave them enough time to for a quick lunch, something light and refreshing. It was the only time Eloy ever saw Bonner ever eat fruit.

They changed their socks and shoes, preparing for the match. It always helped to wash your feet and change your socks and shoes between rounds if you were given the chance. It refreshed your whole body.

It was something Eloy had learned from Bonner. Eloy would have never thought of things like that, but Bonner knew all the tricks.

Bonner said he thought of the feet thing on the square too, which meant he probably didn't. Thinking of something on the square meant you weren't under the influence of alcohol or drugs or in heat. He just didn't want everyone to think the only time he had a good idea was when he was blowing on a roach.

Eloy knew if he were to smoke some marijuana, "blow a roach" as he called it, he would only think of something weird. No way could he come up with something intelligent.

The afternoon match was against two players from Borger, Texas: Reed and Coffey.

The way it turned out, either team that Saturday afternoon could have beaten any team in the tournament.

Any team who would have played against Eloy and Bonner or against Reed and Coffey would have been beaten.

It wouldn't have made any difference if it had been Palmer and Nicklaus.

The first seven holes produced three birdies by Coffey and Reed and two birdies by Baines and Bennet.

After the seventh hole, Eloy and Bonner were two points down.

Then beginning on the eighth hole, each team either birdied or eagled every hole, eight through eighteen. On some holes, there were multiple birdies and eagles.

The scoring went like this:

> Hole # 8: Par-Five.
> Coffey 4, Reed 3. Baines 4, Bennet 4.
> Baines and Bennet—4 down.

> Hole # 9. Par-Four.
> Coffey 4, Reed 3. Baines 3, Bennet 4.
> Baines and Bennet—4 down.

> Hole # 10. Par-Three.
> Coffey 2, Reed 3. Baines 3, Bennet 2.
> Baines and Bennet—4 down.

> Hole # 11. Par-Four.
> Coffey 4, Reed 4. Baines 3, Bennet 3.
> Baines and Bennet—2 down.

> Hole # 12. Par-Four.
> Coffey 3, Reed 4. Baines 4, Bennet 3.
> Baines and Bennet—2 down.

> Hole # 13. Par-Four.
> Coffey 4, Reed 3. Baines 3, Bennet 4.
> Baines and Bennet—2 down.

> Hole # 14. Par-Five.
> Coffey 4, Reed 3. Baines 4, Bennet 5.
> Baines and Bennet—4 down.

> Hole # 15. Par-Four.
> Coffey 3, Reed 3. Baines 3, Bennet 3.
> Baines and. Bennet—4 down.

Hole # 16. Par-Four.
Coffey 3, Reed 4. Baines 4, Bennet 3.
Baines and Bennet—4 down.

Hole # 17. Par-Three.
Coffey 3, Reed 3. Baines 2, Bennet 3.
Baines and Bennet—2 down.

Eloy and Bonner had a hard time believing what was happening. Through the seventeenth hole, Eloy was seven under par and Bonner was six under par.

On the eighteenth tee, Bonner said, "I thought we were dead coming to the seventeenth four down. Your nonfavorite hole and you make a fucking two. Golf is a weird-assed sport, ain't it?"

Bonner also told Eloy that the way this was going, it might take two eagles for them to win the two points necessary for a tie.

Eloy wasn't sure. He thought if they made two eagles, it might only give them a tie on the hole and a loss in the match. An uphill battle for sure.

Eloy was almost right. All four players hit solid, long tee balls into the middle of the eighteenth fairway. All shots were long enough for each player to reach the green in two and have a putt for an eagle.

They all hit their second shots; only Bonner reached the putting surface.

Reed and Coffey both chipped close enough for easy birdies.

Eloy had a delicate chip from the back of the green to the hole located on the front of the green.

When he hit it, he knew it was the perfect speed.

He watched it roll . . . and roll . . . and roll . . . then trickle its way to the hole. It was on the perfect line to go into the cup.

Eloy jumped up into the air when the ball hit the cup and disappeared. He was shocked when the ball came out the other side and stopped an inch from the hole. He had almost made the eagle they needed.

Coffey laughed and shook his head as he picked up the ball and tossed it back to Eloy.

Reed quietly clapped his hands.

Bonner had a twelve-foot putt for an eagle. If he could make it, he could tie the match. The match would then be settled by a sudden-death playoff.

The golf course superintendent, Dude Kincaid, had already started the water sprinklers on the front nine.

Bonner saw him driving up the fairway. Bonner waved to him to come to the eighteenth green.

When Dude drove up, Bonner said, "Turn off those fucking sprinklers. This thing is goin' extra holes!"

Reed and Coffey started laughing, so did Eloy, Dude and some others standing around the green.

Bonner didn't laugh. He waited for the others to quit laughing, and then he calmly stepped up to the putt, settled over the ball, and without any hesitation stroked the ball.

As soon as he hit it, Eloy knew he had made the putt.

When it went in the hole for the eagle, Reed and Coffey laughed even harder.

So did Eloy.

"I'll be damned," said Dude.

"I'll be damned," said Eloy.

"Had it all the way," said Bonner.

Bonner had given them another chance to win the match by making the eagle. It was now a sudden-death playoff and a large crowd had gathered.

On the first extra hole, all players hit solid drives; all found the fairway.

Eloy hit the worst second shot of the group. It was a long way from the hole, in the range of twenty-five feet, a poor shot with only a pitching wedge to the green.

Bonner told Eloy as they drove to the green, "Don't break that club. It wasn't its fault."

Eloy was the first to putt. He stuck the putt perfectly—perfect line and perfect speed. Birdie!

Reed and Coffey both missed their attempts for a birdie. Bonner and Eloy had never led in the entire match and now had won the match!

Eloy said to Coffey as they shook hands, "You know, Jackie, golf is a weird-assed game, ain't it?"

Coffey grinned and shook his head in agreement and then said, "You know, I just can't feel bad about this. I've never shot a sixty-four before and got beat. That was the best match and the best golf I have ever seen in my entire life!"

"Best I was ever around," said Bonner.

"Me too," said Reed. "Does anyone realize how low we shot? Hell, we could have beaten anyone out here today."

Someone in the crowd said, "I think it was four sixty-fours, if I counted right."

All those who had been a witness were in agreement.

Now Eloy and Bonner were in the consolation finals—once again.

So what to do on a Saturday night? Maybe they would be off to Stumpy's for some libations, then maybe to a place like The Pendulum Lounge for a steak and more libations. Life was simple in Amarillo, Texas.

It was at The Pendulum Lounge that evening that Eloy learned the details of Spook's divorce.

Some patron at Stumpy's had mentioned to Spook, in a casual conversation, that whenever he started to play bad he would sneak off out of town somewhere and have sex with a fat girl. He said it was the only cure for the Yips he'd ever found.

The Yips, you know, when your hands go to shaking and they get a mind of their own and won't do what your brain tells them to do. And you look like a stupid fool when you try to putt.

He told Spook the fatter the girl, the better—the longer the spell would last.

Spook told the patron he didn't know if it would work for him or not. He said he used to take Velma out behind The Sixteenth Avenue

Lounge and screw her in the back seat of his Mercedes and for the life of him he couldn't remember that it was ever any help.

The patron said he knew Velma and she was fat enough but she was ugly. He said it had to be with a pretty fat girl. He said you had to be careful and not get a pretty semi-fat girl or an ugly fat girl because it could back fire on a guy. Your yips would continue, and you would catch a case of the duck hooks. That's probably what had happened with Velma, the patron elaborated.

So Spook got to thinking about it and wondered where and with whom Bonner was doing his screwing, because Bonner never had the yips.

"Yeah," said Eloy, "we'll have to follow him sometime."

Spook, being enlightened with Coors Light, figured he could save himself a lot of time and expense money if he could just get the cure at home. His wife was certainly pretty, but the problem was she was also thin. So one night, still enlightened, he explained the theory to his wife, omitting the patron's name to protect the innocent.

She thought he was just being stupid.

Then Spook told her that he didn't want to be out fooling around just to putt well or to cure his pop fly foul right shot, and of course, she agreed. So then Spook asked her if she would mind gaining about forty or fifty pounds.

Well, she didn't think that was such a good idea and also didn't think it was sane to even ask her to do such a thing. And she told him so in so many carefully chosen words; the last sentence ended with "and fuck you too!"

"That must have taken some guts to ask. You must have been wearing your cleats all through this conversation," remarked Eloy.

"Yeah," said Bonner, "that took some balls."

Spook told him, "Come to think of it, I think I was wearing my spikes. But in case you two Einsteins don't know, there is a difference between having guts and having balls. Having guts is coming home after a late night of drinking with the boys and being met by your wife at the door, and she's holding a broom. So you ask her, 'You still cleaning, or you just flying off somewhere!'"

Beer thirty, thought Eloy.

"Now having balls," Spook said, "requires a lot more fortitude. Having balls is when you've been out all night carousing, you got lipstick on your collar, you've got pool cue dust all over your new pants, and you smell like that cheap perfume they use in them strip joints. You wife meets you at the door, you kiss her on the cheek, slap her on the ass, and say, 'You're next, chubby.'"

Bonner remarked that Spook must be talking from experience.

Eloy was laughing.

Then it happened, Spook said, changing the subject back to his explanation of his breakup. For no known reason, none he could lay a finger on, he started playing good. He turned in a couple of seventy-nines and an eighty and then a seventy-six. He slipped up one night after an overload at Stumpy's and said something about it.

Well, she hadn't gained any weight, so the light bulb went on in her head and she confronted him.

Of course, he denied having done anything with anyone, especially a fat girl.

She said, "Bullshit." She had, for years, been hearing all of the rumors, and she knew he hadn't been spending any time at the driving range. "Stumpy's doesn't have range balls," she said. She had this feeling all along he'd been messing around on her, but this episode was the last straw. She couldn't really prove anything, but there was no way he could suddenly shoot a seventy-six unless it was true. "You are not that talented," she said. She just knew he was out flopping around on some fat girl. She said she had done everything in the world to make him happy except leave him. So she made him happy.

He said her parting words were, "I've stirred my last batch of gravy for you, you sorry bastard! No, excuse me, you're not sorry. You're below sorry, whatever that is."

When she left, she told Spook that another thing that bothered her was that he seldom lasted long enough during sex for her to climax.

Spook's only comment was, "Well, I don't know what your problem is. I mean hell, Gina, we both start at the same time, don't we?"

Of course, that was a huge problem for Spook—his wife was not named Gina.

Spook said they went the marriage counselor route but that didn't help either. He said it only lasted one short session. When they met with the counselor the first time, the conversation went something like this.

Counselor: "Well, Mr. and Mrs. Thompson, let's see if we can find some common ground to get you two back on track. Tell me, Mr. Thompson, what do you think you two have in common?"

Spook said he thought for a few minutes and replied, "Let's see. I work. She doesn't. I don't do shopping. I hunt. I don't go to afternoon tea. I go to Stumpy's. I don't paint my fingernails or toenails and I don't get my hair fixed. I get it cut. I don't wear panty hose, or makeup or lipstick. I don't wear high-heel pumps. I wear metal spikes. I don't play bridge. I don't talk to my mother for hours on the phone. I like sex. She doesn't."

"Not with you anyways, not anymore," she interrupted, giving Spook that squinty-eyed, smirking face.

Spook continued, not fazed by her comment. "I like golf. She doesn't. I like my friends. She doesn't. I like it medium rare. She's a well-done. I guess the only thing we completely have in common is *Walker, Texas Ranger* and that neither one of us likes to suck dick!"

Spook said the counselor went into an uncontrollable coughing spasm. His wife jumped out of her chair, took a swing at him, and then left the room.

For the consolation championship match on Sunday, Eloy and Bonner were playing against two teenagers. The two teenagers were college roommates from the Hardin Simmons's golf team.

The consolation final match was normally scheduled for thirty-six holes, just like the championship final. However, each year the head golf professional would get the two teams in the consolation finals to agree to make it an eighteen-hole match so the championship finals would draw more of the attention and most of the crowd.

When the pro asked Eloy and Bonner if they were in agreement, they replied yes.

When he asked the two college boys, they were not in agreement. The college boys wanted to play all thirty-six holes. They were thinking since Eloy and Bonner were older, and out of shape when compared to them, that they could wear them down and win the match during the last eighteen holes.

They made two mistakes in their planning. The first was Eloy and Bonner weren't out of shape, anyway not for playing golf. And the second mistake was the college boys chose to walk and carry their bags, instead of taking a golf cart.

Cassie joined Eloy and Bonner for the final nine holes on Sunday.

When Cassie drove up in her golf cart, Bonner said to Eloy, "Don't pay no never mind to her, bub. We still got business to do. The focus is on the golf. You can focus her later."

It wasn't as good a match as they had had on Saturday afternoon. It couldn't be. There might not be another match that good in the Ross Rogers tournament ever.

This particular day, the two college boys were no match for Baines and Bennet.

One, Eloy and Bonner had all of the confidence working from the day before. And two, the college boys made the mistake of not taking the golf cart. They were even cocky enough not to take it for the last eighteen holes.

Thirty-six holes walking in the Texas panhandle heat wore down a person pretty fast.

Eloy and Bonner played as fast as they could and walked those college boys to death. Eloy and Bonner were always waiting for them on the tee, on the second shot, and on the green. And while Eloy and Bonner waited, they rested and planned their shots.

The college boys were so rushed they didn't have time to plan or to catch their breath.

Eloy wondered why they didn't slow down and make him and Bonner wait. It would have been a good strategy.

After the thirty-first hole, Eloy and Bonner were ahead by seven points. Since each hole was worth two points, there were only ten points remaining to be won.

The fourteenth hole was a dogleg-right par-five guarded by water on the right side of the landing area. The green was located to the right behind the water hazard.

Eloy was in the fairway, waiting to hit. He and Bonner could both reach the green with their second shots. Bonner's ball was lying about ten yards ahead of Eloy's ball.

Eloy's tee ball always looked better when it was in the air than did Bonner's ball, but Bonner's ball always went farther. It was something that mystified Eloy.

"You gonna hit that one iron?" asked Bonner.

"It's gonna be the best one iron I ever hit."

Eloy settled into his stance and was looking back and forth to the green, checking his alignment.

He was distracted by Cassie parking her cart behind the green. He backed off and started over. Eloy took dead aim with his one iron and made as good a swing as he had made all day, and the ball rocketed on a straight line for the green.

He just stood and watched it. Damn, it was pretty.

The ball landed on a sprinkler head and bounced hard. It hit the back fender of the golf cart Cassie was sitting in and then miraculously careened onto the edge of the green.

The two college boys looked at Eloy and shook their heads.

Eloy shrugged his shoulders and said, "How would you have played it?"

Eloy and Bonner won both points on the fourteenth hole. The match was over. It was time to pass out the trophy, collect the money, have a beer, and celebrate.

Eloy and Bonner had won the consolation bracket again, won it handily.

It was the fourth time for Eloy to be on the winning team in the consolation finals.

Cassie was kind and gave the two boys a ride back to the clubhouse in her cart. It was an extra treat for them. They got to watch Cassie's tits bounce up and down on the bumpy fairway. They bought the beer in appreciation for the ride—and the view. They were also happy because it wasn't a pleasant walk when it was long, and hot, and you were the loser.

"Well, we made a check," said Bonner, drinking his first beer.

"Better than nothing, I guess. Don't take offense, but I'm not coming back to the Ross," said Eloy.

"Why not?" asked Cassie and Bonner in unison.

"You can stick a fork in me. I'm done. I'm retiring undefeated in the consolation bracket. I've been in the consolation bracket four times, four victories, no losses. At least it's some kind of record."

"So if they have a Ross Rogers Hall of Fame, your plaque will say, BEST NONWINNER?" asked Cassie.

Eloy grinned, grabbed Cassie around the waist, and said, "Now aren't you just the cutest little thing? Careful, or I'll have to screw you 'till you're mute."

"Well, that can't happen, you know."

"Really . . . And why is that?"

"As long as it would take you, you would lapse into a coma."

"She's telling the truth there, Breeze," said Bonner laughing.

"Anyway, E, I think you should keep playing. You know what they say. 'The pain of losing is temporary, but the glory of winning is forever.'"

Bonner, Eloy, and Cassie walked to the Ross Roger's parking lot together. They passed Dancing D. Dan who was in the process of packing his car for the trip back to Lubbock.

Dancing D. and Roone had lost in the championship finals to the Amarillo Country Club champion and his partner.

Triple J was conversing with Dancing D.

Bonner stopped to talk with them. All three of them enjoyed Cassie's backside as she walked down the parking lot to her car.

"You two wondering what I am?" asked Bonner.

"I can't speak for anyone but me, but the butt be fine," said Triple J. "I don't think it all oughta be just for a pencil dick like the Breeze though. Bitch oughta be into sharing. Dig me? I could help her know what it feels like to have enough to hit bottom."

"So you think all white boys are pencil dicks?" asked Bonner.

"All but Spook," said Triple J. "Spook may be white, but he be paranormal, and so is his dick. I seent a Shetland pony staring at him one time when he was taking a piss."

Bonner pointed at Cassie's ass. "Wouldn't you like to just crawl up in there and eat that sum-bitch raw?" he said, grinning.

"Oh no," said Dancing D. "Fuckin' is fine, but black people don't eat pussy. Nuh uh, no way."

"Yeah, bullshit, why the hell not?" Bonner said unbelievingly.

"Shiiiit Bon-Yay," said Triple J. "Dancing D. be right. We don't puts our tongue on the puss-ey."

"You don't, huh? Well, why the hell not?"

"It's too close to the big nasty, that's why," said Dancing D.

Bonner started laughing like hell. "The big nasty?"

"Yeah, like it be too close to the bunger for my tongue to hunger. Right? Goddamn right!" Triple J laughed as he and Dancing D. slapped hands behind their backs.

Then Triple J said, "El Bon-Yay, do you know the difference between black pussy and a bowling ball?"

Bonner continued to laugh and just shook his head no.

"If you just had to, just absolutely had to, if it was a matter of life and death, if a muthafucka was holdin' a gun to your head, you could eat a fuckin' bowling ball."

Bonner doubled over with the pain of laughter.

CHAPTER 9

Eloy was in The Bar enjoying one of their world famous green chile cheeseburgers for lunch. He was with Himey, R.T., and Ellis Budde.

Three nice, well-built, very young women came into the bar area and passed in front of their table.

"Mmmm, mmmmm, mmmmmum," said R.T., shaking his head.

"How would you like to have some of that?" said Eloy.

Jane, the bartender, overheard and replied, "Wouldn't be that good. They probably wouldn't know how to use it."

"Yeah, but it would be just like getting a new puppy," said Eloy. "Think of all the tricks you could teach 'em. Roll over, fetch, stay, and sit up and beg for a bone."

Himey told them Dallas was irritated that he was going to lunch alone with his friends. He said she told him he was more interested in his friends than in finding the soul mate.

He told her his friends were his soul mates and they were my buds. "Hell, you can't find friends like these just anywhere. Any of them would take a bullet for me or give me their last dollar. Friends like that are hard to find. We have our arguments, fights, throw shit at each other, but you don't ever see us in divorce court! Let me tell you the difference between women friends and men friends. A woman didn't come home one night. The next morning, she told her husband that she had slept over at a friend's house. The man called his wife's ten best friends. None of them knew anything about it. Now here's the difference. A man didn't come home one night. The next morning, he told his wife that he had slept over at a friend's house. The woman called her husband's ten best friends. Eight confirmed that he had slept over, and two said he was still there. Can't replace good friends like that, but as Eloy said, you can find a whole damned gymnasium full of women wanting a scholarship!"

Eloy drove to Clovis, New Mexico, to play in the Colonial Park Country Club Member-Guest. He was the guest of Larry Cummings. Larry was one of the better players in Clovis. It was one of Eloy's favorite golf tournaments.

Eloy left Midland very early and arrived in Clovis before nine in the morning on Friday, the first day of the tournament.

He went to the Ranchers and Farmers Café, one of his favorites, for breakfast.

After he finished breakfast, he went to the Clovis Municipal Golf Course to see Billy Clyde and get a tune-up with his golf game. Billy Clyde gave him the two thumbs-up.

He was surprised when Billy Clyde told him Bonner was playing in the tournament too. Bonner's partner was Jack Hardy, the country club's owner's son.

Eloy arrived at the country club in plenty of time to stretch and warm up.

Friday's round wasn't what Eloy and Larry Cummings exactly had in mind. They didn't play what anyone would call good golf. They did manage a sixty-six. Their score was aided by two chip shots that found the hole. They were two shots behind Bennet and Hardy.

It was mostly Eloy's fault. He should have come up the day before so he would be more rested. But in his DDT-warped sense, he knew he would only go out carousing and drink too much. *What kind of training regimen is that?*

He only made two birdies on a course he knew like the back of his hand—and neither was on a par-five.

Eloy and Larry were standing at the bar after they completed the first round of the tournament. One of the local car dealers approached.

"Hi, guys, how'd y'all do today?"

Larry said, "Sixty-six. It was okay, but sixty-four is leading."

The car dealer looked at Eloy with a smirk and said as he walked off, "I figured as much. I always thought R.T. or Bonner was doing all the playing on that team."

Larry looked at the car dealer sternly and said, "Guess you didn't hear about the sixty-two, did you?"

"Practice round. Big deal. Got to do it when it matters."

Larry looked at Eloy and said, "Don't pay him any attention. He's just mouthing."

"Fuck him. It'll come full circle someday. He couldn't shoot sixty-two with a pencil," said Eloy.

It was the same car dealer that had said bad words about Eloy during the Eastern New Mexico Invitational.

As the car dealer walked away, Eloy saw Patricia Strong come into the room. She was elegant. Eloy's first thought was that this was the definition of *woman*. But he also thought that about Cassie and Adie. So there were three of them. Wonderful! Or maybe there were four. Oh Jesus Jamie suddenly came to mind.

Eloy got a fresh drink and intercepted her as she made the rounds greeting everyone.

"Eloy, my dear," she said, the words running off of her tongue like honey off of a hot spoon. "I haven't seen you in such a long time. How are you?"

"I'm a lot better now." He was looking her up and down and drinking in her exquisite smell. "Damn, you smell good. You smell like you don't want to be left alone, Patricia."

"I can see you haven't changed a bit, have you, E?"

"Why change when you're as charming as me?"

Patricia gave Eloy one of her polite smiles and then joined another group.

Eloy returned to the bar.

Larry, who had been watching the whole time, said, "Wouldn't you like to rub up against that long enough to bring a blister?"

If he only knew, thought Eloy as he said, "You'd need to have your saddle oiled and your gun greased, now wouldn't you?"

Saturday's second round was a carbon copy of Friday's round. Eloy couldn't make a putt. One good thing though, he did make a ten-foot putt for a par that kept them from having a bogey posted on their card. That putt was a small but significant victory for Eloy—and Larry. They carded a sixty-four.

Larry told him it was coming, just be patient. "I mean, Eloy, you hit every fairway and fifteen greens. How much better can that be?"

Eloy and Larry were seated with Bonner and his wife, Tommie.

Ben and Spook came in with their dates for the evening and came to join Eloy, Larry, and the Bennets at the table.

Eloy remarked to Bonner, "Wonder where they found two light hooks in this town?"

Spook introduced the women. One was named Aquanetta, and the other was Gilletta. The names caused a snicker or two.

There were some polite verbal exchanges about who the women were, questions about their backgrounds and what they did for a living.

Tommie Bennet asked about their lineage.

When they didn't know, Spook told them it meant, "Where did your families come from?"

Aquanetta responded, "San Angelo."

When they left to sit at another table, Tommie Bennet leaned over to Eloy and said, "BAFO."

Eloy raised his eyebrows, indicating he didn't know what BAFO meant.

"Brains already fucked out," whispered Tommie. "Neither IQ is even close to room temperature."

They were enjoying the company and the dinner that evening when the rude car dealer approached Eloy. "I guess I'm right. You just can't play without some really good player carrying you, can you? I didn't know Cummings was that good."

Eloy stopped eating. His face was as red as a pickled beet. He got pissed off. "You know if I was as good as you want me to be, I wouldn't be in a one-horse town having to listen to fucks like you. You want some of me on your own?"

"Maybe, if you give me my handicap."

Eloy rose from his chair.

"What's your handicap? Your stupid fucking grin?"

Tommie Bennet knew what was next. She reached over and grabbed Eloy's hand to keep him from hitting the car dealer.

Before the car dealer could reply, Larry said, "His handicap is that he's ugly and he's stupid." Now Larry was irritated too. In the car dealer's attempt to degrade Eloy, he also insulted Larry and ruined a peaceful dinner. Larry slowly folded his napkin and rose from his chair.

The car dealer knew it was time to exit, so he hurriedly left.

So did Eloy. Without finishing his meal, Eloy got up, drank down his scotch, and threw his napkin angrily on the table. He left the club and drove to the Holiday Inn.

He was so mad that he didn't even drink for the rest of the night. He just practiced his putting on the hotel carpet until midnight. Then he fell asleep—still pissed off.

Eloy was awake the next morning and was watching the news in his room when the phone rang.

It was Billy Clyde. All he said was, "Eight inches past the hole, not six, not ten." And then he hung up.

Larry and Eloy were in the next-to-last group on Sunday. They were three shots behind Bonner and Hardy.

On the first hole, Eloy hit it six feet from the hole. He missed the putt.

On the second hole, a long par-three measured at 210 yards, Eloy hit it four feet from the hole.

Larry was in the bunker to the left of the green. He blasted out to six feet but then missed the putt for his par.

It was Eloy's turn to putt. It was unbelievable. He three-putted! You could see the anger rise from his shirt collar to his visor. He clenched his jaw but didn't say a word. But you could hear his teeth cracking.

Then he saw Billy Clyde. It reminded him of what he needed to do. *Concentrate, damn it.*

On the third hole, a short par-four, Eloy hit this approach shot to five feet. But it was another missed opportunity. Eloy and Larry walked off the fourth green with only a par.

On the fourth hole, again, Eloy hit it to five feet. But as the holes before, it was another miss.

Eloy got in the cart and said, "I'm trying hard as I can."

Larry didn't say anything.

On the fifth hole, a par-five, Eloy hit his best drive of the week, aided by some anger. For his second shot to the par-five, he then hit a rocket two iron that landed just short of the green and rolled to fifteen feet from the hole. He had a nice makeable putt for an eagle. A problem for Eloy was he was above the hole and the putt broke to the left—the worst kind of putt for him.

Larry missed his birdie putt and tapped in for his par.

Now it was Eloy's turn to try for the eagle.

Larry stood behind Eloy's ball and surveyed the line.

"What do you think?" Larry asked him. "Foot and a half, and little speedy?"

Eloy agreed, settled in, took a deep breath, and said under his breath, "Okay, eight inches." He stroked the putt as smoothly as he could, like Billy Clyde had told him. It slowly trickled down the small slope and disappeared into the hole. Eagle three!

"What happened? You made one," said Larry.

"It was a voodoo putt."

"A voodoo putt?"

"A fucking voodoo putt, magic man. Hit it, and *poof!* Right in the hole for an eagle."

"Black magic?"

"White magic, my friend. White voodoo fucking magic."

Eloy's least favorite hole on Colonial Park Country Club was the sixth hole. It is a dogleg-right, opposite of Eloy's natural draw. There was water on the left and lots of trees on the right. This hole always gave Eloy trouble. He hit a good tee shot avoiding the water, then a very good approach shot, and made another putt for a birdie.

On the seventh hole, a par-five, Eloy missed the green to the right and then chipped to within six inches from the hole.

Larry putted first and made a fifteen-foot putt for a birdie.

Nonchalantly, Eloy tapped in for his birdie.

His speed with the putter was now perfect. He didn't have to think about it. He was on automatic.

Larry made another downhill, right to left, putt for birdie on the par-three eighth hole and then birdied number nine.

They were on a roll, as some would say. Suddenly, they were tied for first place. They were tied with Bonner and Hardy heading into the back nine.

It seemed like Eloy was on automatic pilot. He would draw the putter back, stroke the ball, and then the ball would find the hole. Each time, he would say, "Magic. White voodoo magic!"

On the back nine, Eloy made six more birdies—holes ten, twelve, thirteen, fourteen, fifteen, and sixteen. It would have been seven birdies, but he three-putted the last hole, a closing par-five, for a par. But Eloy's three-putt was of no consequence.

Larry birdied the eighteenth hole, giving them a team score of sixty.

Bonner, in the last group, had about a ten-foot putt for a birdie. If he made the putt, his team would tie Eloy and Larry for the tournament. But Bonner missed the putt. In a loud, shrill voice, loud enough for everyone to hear him, he said, "Cocksucker."

The tournament was over and it was made official.

In winning the tournament, Eloy and Larry had just set the new scoring record for the Colonial Park Member-Guest: 190 for three rounds.

Eloy was credited with shooting a new competitive course record of sixty-three.

"Best round I've ever seen you play, E," said Larry. "Just think about those putts on the first few holes. Good god almighty, could have been a fifty-eight or fifty-nine."

"Thanks. There's someone we should find, don't you think?"

Eloy and Larry looked for the car dealer and found him at the bar.

"So what do you think now? Still think someone's been carrying my ass around all these years? I'm available tomorrow if you want to catch me alive and in person," said Eloy.

"Maybe I was wrong. Didn't mean to piss you off." Then the car dealer drank down his beer and left the club.

Eloy said to him as he walked off, "I think you need some more training on how to be a jerk, you loud-mouthed fuck."

"Now, now, now, Eloy. That's no way to talk in high-class establishment like this," said Patricia.

"If it's so high-class, how come he is a member?"

Patricia raised her eyebrows.

"How much you want for this place? I want to buy it just so I can kick his ass out!"

CHAPTER 10

Eloy pulled the Mercedes into the parking lot at La Bodega Cantina at 11:48 a.m. on Monday, the day after the Colonial Park Member-Guest.

He went in the main door and headed upstairs to the lounge. Before his foot hit the top stair, Mary Sue, the bartender, handed him a Miller Lite.

Eloy took his beer and walked back to where he always had lunch.

Himey was standing in front of the men's room door.

"What's up?" Eloy said. "Full house."

"Sonny's poofing some little road runner in there right now."

Poof was a term they used for "plain old ordinary fucking."

"You're kidding?" said Eloy, surprised.

Eloy found Dad and Ellis at the big table in the corner. Dad was eating a green chile cheeseburger. The green chile cheeseburger at La Bodega was one the best in all of the free world, on a par with the green chile cheeseburger at The Bar in downtown Midland—or the green chile cheeseburger at The Owl Café in San Antonio, New Mexico.

Himey joined them and ordered more beer.

Eloy ordered a green-chile cheeseburger, just like Dad's, plus an order of stuffed jalapenos.

Eloy looked around and didn't see John Echard. John was usually at La Bodega on Mondays playing Pac-Man with Himey.

"Anybody seen old Johnny boy lately? I ain't seen him in a couple of weeks, since he got out of the hospital."

"If I see him again, he may go back," answered Ellis.

Dad responded, "I think he's off chasing some assistant pro from Odessa. He thinks he's been porkin' Megan."

"You're kidding," said Eloy.

"Nope. Truth. It would probably be a good idea if you three boys went and made sure that John didn't find that boy."

"Why's that?" asked Ellis.

"'Cause that way the assistant pro can always take the blame for all of the sport fucking she's been doing on the side," Dad said, looking straight at Himey. "Know what I mean, son? We wouldn't want Johnny boy to know the truth, now would we?"

Himey, Ellis, and Eloy all said, "We'll get right on it."

Dad got this sheepish grin on his face and said, "Now which one of you was it that taught her to hold her breath for so long under water?"

That statement dropped like a bomb—a big fucking bomb.

Good god oh mighty, they all thought. *Dad! Dad of all people, got scuba dived by Megan. Son of a bitch, no wonder he had a vested interest in John not finding out the truth.* They all burst out laughing.

"Reckon how all of that came about?" asked Eloy.

"It's your fault," said Dad.

"Oh, so here we go again. Blame Eloy for everything. I guess I started all of the trouble in China too, huh?"

"Yep, the way I heard it told, they put up the Great Wall because of you," said Himey, laughing.

Dad, looking directly at Eloy, changed the subject. "When's your tee time in the city championship this weekend?"

"Couldn't tell you," Eloy replied. "They haven't told us yet."

"It's at one o'clock Saturday," said Ellis. "It's me, you, and a couple of guys I don't know."

"How did you find out?" asked Eloy.

"Pretty difficult," said Budde. "I called and asked."

The Midland City Championship was only a two-day competition, Saturday and Sunday.

The odds-on favorite was the best player in Midland at the time, Billy Francis Doan. Some just called him BFD.

BFD was a hustler and gambler, known to use Carmex on occasion to "lubricate" the face of his driver. When the face of a driver is "lubricated," it produces no spin on the ball. It's a distinct advantage if you're lubricating and your opponent isn't.

R.T. told Eloy about the very first time he ever played golf on a real course. His first time was at a city course in Cleburne, Texas. The day he chose for his first venture happened to be a day when the course was having a tournament. The golf course pro talked R.T. into playing. R.T. informed the group he was assigned to that he had never played golf on a golf course before.

The best player of the group took R.T. to the driving range and watched him hit a few balls. R.T. was very strong as a young man and hit the ball very hard, but unfortunately each one when way to the right. R.T. said the man took some Vaseline and "lubricated" the face of his driver. R.T. said he then hit every shot straight . . . and long.

Their team won the tournament, and that was how R.T. got his first full set of irons. First prize was a set of First Flight irons. All with the complements of Vaseline, Pure Petroleum Jelly!

Saturday, the first day of the city championship, Eloy was paired with Budde and two players he was only vaguely familiar with.

One was a Midland Junior College player, a South African student he knew who worked at Green Tree Country Club.

The other he had only heard of.

Eloy was lucky. He got to ride a cart by himself because the college player chose to walk and Budde was already on the cart with the other player.

He wondered why all college players walked when they had a chance to ride and rest. Some claimed they played better when they walked. He couldn't recall at this particular time ever having lost to one of them who was walking.

Riding alone was good. This way, he didn't have to make small talk with a cart partner.

Another thing Eloy liked was being in the first group to tee off in the Championship Flight.

The round he played that Saturday could only be described as lackluster.

The player riding with Budde was not a championship-caliber player and sometimes that was a problem for the other players. He did not break eighty for the day. Why he was in this flight, Eloy didn't know, unless he was a late entry and was merely flight filler. Every flight had to have its filler. Those players who thought they could play one level above their skills ability but couldn't. Might as well be their money as someone else's. The winner didn't care; he would take it anyway.

Budde didn't play well either, shooting a seventy-six.

Eloy turned in a seventy for the day. He didn't think it would be good enough for him to be in contention. Usually, it took a score in the sixties to be near the lead.

The teenager from South Africa had the best score in the group, a sixty-nine.

No one shot a low score that day, not even BFD.

"Walgreens must be out of Carmex," said Budde when he saw BFD's score.

Eloy was surprised his score of seventy put him in the last group on Sunday. He was paired with R.T., BFD, and the teenager from South Africa. Each of them had shot a sixty-nine.

Eloy had one stroke to make up, which was not insurmountable, but against three players, especially BFD, it made the task much more difficult. Eloy had played BFD many times and lost more than he won. Eloy once shot sixty-five on consecutive days and lost to BFD both times.

Eloy decided that even though R.T. was one of his best friends, this would be one of those days when he wouldn't speak to his competitors. He would just be an elusive, arrogant, nonspeaking asshole, as he was once called. He could do that well—he had practiced it many times.

Of course, to his way of thinking, how could you be an asshole if you didn't talk, didn't throw clubs, minded your own business, were polite, and just played golf? Some people were just fucking weird, he decided. He made a mental note that he would ask Cassie, who majored in psychology, how that could be possible.

Dad always said that business was business and love was horseshit. Well, today was all business and love could just wait until it was dark and there was scotch involved.

For the final round, the teenager from South Africa decided to ride a golf cart instead of walk.

Amazing, thought Eloy. *Hell, he might even graduate.*

The boy deciding to ride caused Eloy a problem though. Eloy didn't want to ride with anyone but was placed on the same cart as BFD. He tried to bribe the pro into letting him ride in a cart by himself, but the pro refused.

So hurriedly, he called Himey to come and caddie for him.

Himey arrived just in the nick of time, rented a spectator cart, loaded up Eloy and his bag, and they headed for the first tee.

Himey could rent a separate cart and Eloy couldn't. Why? Maybe he had been gone too long from the Monday game. It would be another deep subject for Cassie. He sure wished she were here right now.

Eloy never did see reasoning behind it all. Eloy couldn't ride a cart by himself but a spectator could—figure that one out. Maybe the pro didn't want BFD to ride alone. Or maybe it was Eloy who he thought needed supervision. But thanks to Himey though, he did not have to ride with a fellow competitor.

The front nine, on Sunday afternoon, saw the lead change several times. R.T. and BFD were tied after nine holes. Eloy was one shot behind with a solid thirty-four. The teenager from South Africa had fallen behind and would no longer be a factor.

The back nine was going to be interesting. The back nine on this Sunday was being played on the newest nine of the three nines at Hogan Park Municipal Golf Course. It was the best and the hardest nine of the three.

As Eloy stepped up to hit his tee ball on the tenth tee, Dad drove up in another cart.

All he could think about was, *Damn, that cart shit doesn't make any sense at all. Where in the fuck is Cassie when you need her?* With his mind on something other than golf, Eloy hit a bad drive into the mesquites on the left side of the tenth fairway. It pissed him off. He should have stepped back and started over when Dad drove up; he wasn't that stupid, but then he was.

He was looking at a bogey at least, maybe double, and this was the easiest par-four on the back nine. "Stupid motherfucker," he said to himself. Getting pissed off was a good for him. He got focused. He was now in the frame of mind where he should have been all day—in a high state of "miffification," as he called it. In that state, he could block out all of the bullshit, think only of golf, his "Fuck the scenery" state of mind as he called it.

Himey found Eloy's ball.

Eloy saw it and knew the only shot he had was to hit it sideways.

"Stupid motherfucker," he said to himself again.

Eloy studied for a moment, calming down.

He selected his sand wedge and hit the ball to the middle of the fairway.

He then stomped angrily out of the scrub mesquites. "Stupid motherfucker," he said to himself again.

A good thing happened. He now had a perfect lie and was only one hundred yards from the hole.

He selected his pitching wedge, made perfect contact with the ball, and it landed about fifteen feet from the cup.

He wasn't too happy about it. He turned to Himey and spoke for the first time.

"If Bonner ever hit a wedge that bad, he would break its fuckin' neck."

"Yeah, but then he'd be man enough to go and make the putt," said Dad.

Eloy didn't respond or look at Dad as he walked to his cart.

But that's what Eloy did. He made that fifteen-foot putt.

When the ball hit the back of the hole and dropped in the cup for a par, he showed no emotion.

Himey thought he saw him yawn, sort of. So did Dad. If they had been inside his body, they would have seen he was nervous as hell, like the character Don Knotts played on television. They would have also known that he was locked in mentally.

They all made good shots on the eleventh, twelfth, and thirteenth holes. Eloy, R.T., and BFD each made one birdie.

Eloy birdied the fourteenth hole to tie for the lead. R.T. made a bogey by three putting the fourteenth and was now one shot behind.

Eloy and BFD both made birdie on the par-five fifteenth hole.

They were tied for the lead going to the sixteenth hole. The sixteenth hole was the most difficult hole on the golf course. A 425-yard par-four, downhill from the tee, then doglegged to the left. A big bunker guarded the left side of the fairway where it doglegged, and then it was uphill to the green. Water guarded the end of the fairway, just in case you hit too far. Left and right of the fairway was no man's land, a mass of scrub mesquite bushes.

BFD drove first, straight down the left side of the fairway. His line was slightly right of the bunker.

Perfect drive, thought Eloy. As he watched BFD's ball land, it got a bad bounce to the left and landed in the big bunker guarding the left side of the dogleg. Since the fairway sloped a little downhill and to the right, Eloy couldn't imagine how that ball bounced left, but it did!

BFD looked at Eloy as the turned toward his golf cart.

Eloy shrugged his shoulders and said, "I don't know how it did that either."

Eloy drove next. He felt the contact with the ball and looked up to watch the flight. He was shocked. He didn't know why, but his ball was flying right, fading. *Why in hell would I be hitting a fade now?* His temperature rose. *I've been trying all of my adult life to hit a fade with a driver and never have. And now the dirty rotten sum-bitch rears its ugly head. What a crying-out-loud shame.* He was a hooker. What the hell was he doing hitting a fade at this crucial point? Was he choking? Where his ball was heading was to no-man's land, Bogey Ville. He'd rather be in the bunker with BFD.

When he walked to the cart, both Himey and Dad wouldn't look him in the eye, like he was a serial rapist or killer or child molester, and he was glad they didn't.

His ball landed on the edge of the cart path and bounced hard to the right. Then it caught one of the scrub mesquites and jumped farther to the right and disappeared. He was hoping it wasn't in the middle of one of those scrub mesquites. If your ball landed in the middle of one of those scrub mesquites, you were dead. And so was your score for the hole.

They all looked and eventually found the ball, or anyway Himey found it.

Eloy looked to make sure it was his original ball; one never knew what friends might do. He saw the ball had a scuffmark made by the cart path, and it also had the familiar six-dot triangle pattern he used to mark his ball.

He had gotten lucky with where the ball came to rest. He could swing free without hitting any of the scrub bushes. The problem was it was a shot of over 220 yards and he had to flirt with the greenside bunker in order to get it on the green. But at least it was an open shot—even if it was on hardpan.

To make things worse, especially for Eloy, they had to wait. The foursome in front of them had run into some trouble of their own. Eloy went to his ball and stood in the middle of the scrub mesquites and stared at nothing. They had to wait long enough for him to wish he had cigarette. Instead, he stuck a golf tee in his mouth. He could taste the dirt where the tee had been placed in the ground. He thought it tasted sort of like mescal. He wouldn't even mind a shot of mescal right about now. He stood there several minutes.

Himey broke his concentration.

Eloy was thinking about nothing, but he was concentrating on it.

Himey tapped him on the shoulder and handed him his one iron. "You've hit a hundred on the range, bub. One more won't hurt, right over the pole."

The pole Himey referred to was the telephone pole on the old Hogan Park Driving Range where Eloy practiced hitting one irons. He would hit one iron after one iron trying to get it to fly over the pole. On occasion, he could do it several times in a row.

Eloy flipped the fake-cigarette golf tee to the ground. *Too bad it wasn't a real cigarette. It could have caught the mesquites on fire and burned down these stroke-stealing pieces of shit—all of them! It would serve them right. Fuck the sixteenth hole.*

Eloy took a line to the hole so if he missed the shot a little bit it would leave him an easy up and down for his par. He was aiming to avoid the right front bunker.

The bunkers at Hogan Park weren't really bunkers. They didn't have any sand in them, just some loosely packed hardpan and a few small rocks. Hitting explosion shots from them was not easy. As a matter of fact, hitting any shot from them was not easy.

He thought about what Himey just said, of all the times at the Hogan Park driving range when he practiced hitting those one irons off the hardpan and trying to clear the telephone phone. He wanted one, just one, like one of those good ones.

He set his mind for a good, smooth tempo and then put his swing into motion. He felt it first, and then he heard it. Even before he looked up to catch the flight of the ball, he knew he had hit that one iron perfectly . . . right on the sweet spot. The ball rose gently against the bright-blue Texas sky, and then, by damn, it started to fade.

Eloy looked around to see if he was the person who actually hit that shot. *Jack fucking Nicklaus, I might just learn to love that fade.*

The ball landed just on the front of the green, bounced right, almost went in the hole, and stopped six feet from the pin.

To Eloy's astonishment, both R.T. and BFD, yes BFD, clapped.

Eloy shrugged his shoulders, just like he did when BFD's ball bounced sideways into the bunker. And Eloy was surprised. He didn't know BFD had that much sportsmanship about him until right then.

Himey said, "I don't care what you say, it doesn't get any better than that. If you could put tits on it, I would marry it."

Eloy was wishing that one iron did have tits. He'd run away, marry the bitch, and be happy for the rest of his life.

Dad said, "Hoooooly shiiiiit. If you never hit another one, you don't have to!"

Eloy looked at Dad and said, "I hot-jumped that sum-bitch, huh?"

Both Dad and Himey responded, "Amen!"

"Kiss a pussy," Eloy said, and then he grinned for the first time that day.

BFD half-hit, half-topped his shot out of the fairway bunker and into the bunker in front of the green.

He either had a bad lie in the bunker, thought Eloy, *or the one iron had jumped up his ass, grabbed him by the throat, and was choking his ass.*

Eloy missed his six-foot birdie putt and BFD made a double bogey six. Eloy now had a two-shot lead with two holes to play.

Eloy thought he should reconsider, thought that he maybe was wrong. He might just come to love the number sixteen. He had met Cassie, the best woman he'd ever known, at the Sixteenth Avenue Lounge, and now the critical turning point in the tournament had come on the sixteenth hole. Love that number sixteen. How quickly he changed his mind.

The seventeenth hole was a 210-yard par-three. It had an L-shaped green, with water looming on the front right. The pin this Sunday was cut in the front of the green, the narrowest section, where the water came into play the most.

Eloy had the honors and stood there thinking about the last two shots he had hit—both had faded. He took the cautious way out and aimed at the left part of the green. If he hit a hook now, aiming left, he would be back in another mass of scrub mesquites. Luckily for him, he didn't. He hit a four iron and the ball flew straight—no hook, no fade—just to the left front of the green.

BFD hit his approach about ten feet to the right of the hole and then made his putt for a birdie.

Eloy three-putted, missing a three-foot putt for a par. He now had only a one-stroke lead with one hole to play.

BFD had the honors on the eighteenth tee and hit his drive perfectly. You could not have walked it up there and placed it any better.

Eloy wanted to buy it, and he said so.

Eloy hit his tee ball, and as it left the face of his driver, he looked up. He was again astonished. He couldn't believe it. He had hit a fade again! It was headed for the same batch of scrub mesquites that he had found with his errant drive on the sixteenth hole.

Lee Trevino always said you could talk to a fade, and Eloy was talking his ass off.

"Come on, baby, just get clean. Please don't play hide-and-seek. Come on, darlin'. Be kind to Daddy. Candy up, baby, candy up."

Himey was talking to it too, and Dad was actually praying.

When Eloy got back to his cart, he told Himey, "You think something's wrong with this goddamn driver? Or is it the pesky old choke bug?"

Himey only said, "Uh-huh."

Eloy found his ball. He had gotten lucky again. It had somehow gone far enough to be past the last stretch of scrub mesquites, giving him a free swing. His ball was only eighty yards from the green, but it was sitting, again, on nothing but hardpan.

Eloy got agitated. He tried to calm himself by lighting a cigarette. He reached in his bag and found nothing. Again, he forgot he had quit. "Shit," he said.

He looked at Himey. "Doesn't this goddamn place have anything but hardpan? Don't they know you can plant grass in dirt, throw some water on it, and it will grow? Where's the fucking greenskeeper? Huh? Where is he? Out killing some more grass somewhere!"

"Look over there," said Himey, pointing to the fairway. "See that green shit? That's called grass. You can hit it there any time you want to, you know."

Eloy looked hard at Himey. Then he started laughing. It relieved the tension.

Himey said, "Remember Kerrville?"

Eloy nodded. He remembered back to Kerrville, Texas, when he had a similar shot to win the Texas State Four Ball Championship with R.T. as his partner.

He took his Wilson sand wedge, proceeded to his ball, and without hesitation, calmly hit the ball toward the green. The instant the ball left the clubface, Eloy could see it spinning, and he couldn't believe it, but it talked to him. "Look at me spin. Pretty aren't I? But don't worry. Even though you hit me too hard, I'm not gonna fuck you over. Instead, I'm gonna land on the green just above pin high, jump onto the collar to cause you some anxiety, and then spin left toward the hole for an easy putt even an anvil-handed sum-bitch like you can make. And by the way, you're welcome. Just quit hitting me into the weeds."

The Titleist golf ball landed just above the hole as promised. It jumped onto the collar, hesitated, and then spun left and backward, almost going into the hole before stopping six feet away.

BFD hit his ball to twelve feet from the hole. But this time he missed his putt for a birdie.

Two putts later, Eloy was the Midland City champion.

Dad was the first one to congratulate Eloy. "That was some good golf. Sixty-nine, my favorite number."

Eloy smiled and exhaled.

Both BFD and R.T came and offered their hands to Eloy and gave him their congratulations.

Eloy and Himey did the high five and the knuckle bump and then jumped into the golf cart and headed for the pro shop. Cold beer was in order. Eloy wished the cart would go faster. So did Himey.

As they rounded the corner from the eighteenth green toward the clubhouse, Eloy saw a pair of women leaning against one of the picnic tables under the concrete veranda that fronted the pro shop. One of them was Dallas Syntrele. The other one was wearing a white sleeveless blouse, blue jeans, ropers, and a baseball cap with Texas embroidered in burnt orange across the front. She had her hair in a ponytail, Eloy's favorite style.

Eloy knew instantly who she was. It was Cassie Ann Channing.

Eloy said to Himey, "Ah, trophies to be claimed. We are two lucky dudes, huh?" said Eloy.

"Huh!" replied Himey.

Himey stopped the golf cart, jumped out, and gave Cassie a hug. Then he and Dallas went inside to get them a beer.

Eloy grabbed Cassie and gave her a big, long kiss.

When they separated, she said, "I guess you won, huh?"

"Scraped it around, but somehow I got it done. A victory for The Breeze!"

Cassie looked at Eloy and gave him her best smile. "And I bet somewhere along the line you had to hit a hard one iron off a bare dirt lie, didn't you?"

Eloy smiled from ear to ear. "Yeah, as a matter of fact I did. That and a sand wedge. Who told you?"

"Maybe you should only play golf courses where you have to hit one irons on every hole. Hell, E, you'd win every one then."

"Cassie, you can't tempt fate that many times. Hitting one irons is just like hard-ons. You're only allotted so many in your life, and you have to make the best use of them as you can. So you can't use 'em up all at one time. You got to spread 'em out."

Cassie laughed. "You'll never change, will you? Golf, whiskey, and sex."

"What the hell else is there? Only way it could get better is if all this had background music."

"I guess if there were, they'd be playing 'We Are the Champions,' huh?"

"Something like that."

"You really like that name don't you, E.B. Breeze?"

"Suits me well."

Eloy placed his hand on Cassie's thigh and started moving his hand back and forth.

Cassie said, "Now E, don't you know by now that I'm like a M&M. I melt in your mouth, not in your hand."

"Works for me," said Eloy.

"Well, how 'bout we finish this beer, go get a room at the Hilton, get naked and make love, and break up some furniture."

"Make love," Eloy said, raising his eyebrows. "You said 'make love'?"

Cassie nodded her head in agreement.

"So let's see. We've progressed from fancy fucking to screwing to making love? Does that mean we're gonna get married now?"

Cassie gave Eloy a gentle kiss. "There you go."

"Why go to the Hilton and not at my house?"

"Then we won't have to furniture shop tomorrow. And by the way, if we do get married I'm going to change my name to C.C. Breeze."

On Wednesday, August 6, Eloy called his father.

It was his father's birthday.

Eloy was extremely proud of himself. This whole summer had been magical—the best ever.

"Hello, Pop. Happy birthday!"

"Thanks, son. What you been up to?"

"Well, I won the Midland City Championship, and I've decided to get married!"

There was a long pause.

"That's good, son. Congratulations on both. Is she pregnant?"

Eloy laughed. "No, Pop. It's Cassie, the one I've been telling you about."

"Bless her sweet heart."

CHAPTER 11

Eloy and Cassie decided to fly to Las Vegas to get married. They invited all of their friends. It was going to be one grand party.

"Most of the guys tell me they don't want to play golf when we get to Vegas."

"Now that is scary."

"Scares me, and I'm fearless," said Eloy. "What do you suppose happens if you get scared half to death twice?"

"Nothing, I would think."

"Really? Don't two halves make a whole? You'd be deader than hell."

"Nope, wouldn't happen."

"Okay, explain this one to me."

"C'mon, E, you're smarter than this. Look, if you had fifty years of your life left and you were scared half to death, then you would have twenty-five years left. Keep dividing by two and so on. You'd have to be scared half to death a hell of a lot of times for it to really happen."

"You're too fucking cerebral sometimes, know that?"

"There you go!"

On the plane to Las Vegas, Cassie asked Eloy, "So what do you think we'll being doing to keep the excitement going even when we're old?"

"Oh you mean like next year or when we're fifty or so?"

"Yeah, fifty is old and decrepit, isn't it?"

"Sounds ancient to me."

"Reckon we'll even be doing it then?"

"You mean sex? Heck, I don't know. Dad is sixty-five and he still gets it all the time."

"Yeah, Sylvia told me he is still in overdrive. She said you'd think that after forty years or so a lady wouldn't have to have sex three or four times a week. She said that wasn't what she really signed on for."

"Well, she could always get him a surrogate fucker now, couldn't she?"

"Sylvia? You know she mentioned that. She said she was looking for someone to come in on Tuesdays and clean the house and then clean out Dad's pipes."

"Any taker's yet?"

"She had one, but seems she run off with some assistant golf pro from Odessa."

Eloy chose not to comment; instead, he got back to the subject of being old.

"I'm guessing we'll just sit around in an E-Z-Boy recliner and watch TV every night, do crossword puzzles and shit. Probably the only thing we'll use whipped cream for is to put on our sugar-free Jell-O."

"No excitement at all, huh?"

"I guess for excitement we could sprinkle some crushed pecans on top."

"I don't like pecans."

"You *are* going to be bored, aren't you?"

"So can you think of any other way to keep the magic?"

"Marry a magician, I reckon."

Himey, R.T., Ben, Bonner, Spook, Stan, Bubba, and Ellis all stood and drunkenly witnessed the death of Eloy, notorious, not famous, Eloy Baines—and the christening of Mr. Married Baines, the Eloy Baines now with two names on his checkbook.

Himey tried to tell him to get Cassie her own checking account and leave his alone, but here Eloy was, thinking with the small head again.

They were all surprised Eloy was really going to give up his bachelor status, but then they also knew that Eloy once said fidelity was only a stereo component. They would have laughed and thought it fitting if they knew the marriage certificate was in the name of E.B. and C.C. Breeze!

They, along with girlfriends and wives, some with both, had flown to Las Vegas compliments of a private plane paid for with Eloy's credit card.

Eloy would discover that fact at the end of the month when the credit card bill would come in the mail and all of his neighbors would hear him screaming!

"I can't believe Eloy is actually committing to this monotonous relationship," said Ben to R.T. and Kathy.

Kathy looked at Ben with a sour look on her face. "It's a *monogamous* relationship, not *monotonous,* stupid."

"Same difference," said Ben.

R.T. grinned. Kathy didn't.

"See, Kathy, variety is the spice of life. Eloy is giving that up," continued Ben. "Just like your food, you wouldn't want to eat the same old thing every meal, with the same old spices on it, would you? You know you'd need to put a little something on tofu to help it out."

"It isn't the same. Tell him, R.T."

"Wait a second, R.T. don't need to get in trouble over this, Kathy. This is 'tween me and you. All I'm saying is, you just need a little paprika here and some parsley there, that's all. I never found one woman like that yet and I've been through my share. Some are steak. Some are chicken! They're both good to eat, but they taste different, and I don't want to have either one every day."

Ben showed up at the selected wedding chapel with two showgirls, in full regalia, and introduced them as The Spinner Twins.

Eloy called them Roulette and Baccarat. They wore spangled-red-sequined suits, what there was of them, with the fishnet hose and red high-heel fuck-me shoes. They had on showgirl headdresses with the gold helmet and black, red, and white plumes coming out of the top. The plumes stood about two feet tall.

Spook Thompson said they were the best he had ever been around. Better than the ones they took to Clovis. When pressed for the details, Spook said it wasn't proper to talk about the sexual appetites of his and Ben's next wives. He did say, however, that when the one Eloy called Baccarat had a climax, she would cry, and Spook liked that.

When Cassie walked into the chapel, she noticed a set of golf clubs sitting in the back corner. The first person she saw was R.T. Deacon. "R.T., what in the world are those doing here?" she said pointing toward the golf clubs. "I thought you guys played all of your golf this morning."

R.T. looked at Cassie with a big smile and said, "This ain't gonna take all day, is it?"

Cassie looked over at Eloy, and he just shrugged his shoulders and gave her one of his shit-eating grins.

They all played golf that morning for the last time with Eloy as a free man. But deep down, they all knew this wouldn't change him. As Eloy had said more than once, old dogs don't change the way they trot. You see, during the ceremony, they looked at Eloy's feet, and he was still wearing his golf shoes.

They all left to drink and gamble,
Inexorably bound as friends,
The circuit goes in a forever circle,
And the party never ends!

A few days later, Cassie and Eloy ventured to Mesquite, Nevada. It was one of the few places where prostitution was legal, and Eloy said it would be a shame to not do some exploration. They found a nice hotel, Eloy parked the car in the spot marked New Registrations Only, and went inside.

The hotel clerk was a girl in her twenties. She smiled as Eloy approached the registration desk.

"Hi, young lady, do you have any vacancies?"

"Let me see," responded the clerk. She checked her computer screen and announced, "Yes, we do."

"Give me the best room you have."

"Is this a special occasion, sir?"

"Yes, ma'am. I just got married."

"Oh, would you like the bridal?"

Eloy couldn't resist. He gave the clerk a big smile and said, "No, that's okay. I'll just hold her by her ears until she gets used to it!"

Epilogue

Some of the records set in that era of the Bar-B-Que Circuit will never be broken. Some courses have had dramatic changes, most for the worst, and some have simply closed.

The Bar-B-Que Circuit still exists today, but in different formats and different courses with different characters, but none as colorful as those I encountered.

One of the main reasons I worked was so I could play those events. I might have made more money had I done things differently. But I would not take any amount of money in exchange for the experiences I had.

It defined me as who I am. As with Eloy, it is what makes me tick. I love it still.

Photos

From the Circuit

Roy Deaton, Ed Barnes, Spencer Harrell, and Ben Brock.

Jimmie Wilson, Ed Barnes, and Captain Jay Ellis.